When they hit the dance floor, Judd pulled London snug against his body.

Wrapping one arm around her slender waist, he reached up with his other arm to tuck her head against his shoulder. Her breath warmed his skin through the thin material of his shirt.

He rested his cheek against her bright hair and the golden strands stuck to the stubble of his beard. Reaching between their bodies, he opened her leather jacket and drew her close again, his chest pressing against her soft breasts beneath the silvery material of her dress.

She shifted and her soft lips touched the side of his neck.

He gritted his teeth to suppress the shudder threatening to engulf his body...and for the first time in a very long time and a very long line of women, he felt on the edge of losing control.

Then the door to the bar burst open and London's driver, bloodied and battered, staggered into the room and dropped to the floor.

THE HILL

—

CAROL ERICSON

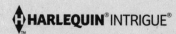
HARLEQUIN® INTRIGUE®

Recycling programs
for this product may
not exist in your area.

To all the ladies at GIAMx2

ISBN-13: 978-0-373-69790-8

THE HILL

This edition published by arrangement with Harlequin Books S.A.

For questions and comments about the quality of this book, please contact us at CustomerService@Harlequin.com.

® and TM are trademarks of Harlequin Enterprises Limited or its corporate affiliates. Trademarks indicated with ® are registered in the United States Patent and Trademark Office, the Canadian Intellectual Property Office and in other countries.

Printed in U.S.A.

ABOUT THE AUTHOR

Carol Ericson lives with her husband and two sons in Southern California, home of state-of-the-art cosmetic surgery, wild freeway chases, palm trees bending in the Santa Ana winds and a million amazing stories. These stories, along with hordes of virile men and feisty women, clamor for release from Carol's head. It makes for some interesting headaches until she sets them free to fulfill their destinies and her readers' fantasies. To find out more about Carol, her books and her strange headaches, please visit her website, www.carolericson.com, "Where romance flirts with danger."

Books by Carol Ericson

HARLEQUIN INTRIGUE

‡Brothers in Arms
§Guardians of Coral Cove
**Brothers in Arms: Fully Engaged
ΩBrody Law

CAST OF CHARACTERS

Judd Brody—A private investigator whose current client, an heiress with a stalker, proves to be more than he bargained for, both professionally and personally. But their pasts are intertwined, and helping her just might help him solve the mystery of his father's suicide.

London Breck—This socialite heiress has a lot on her plate; what she doesn't need is someone stalking her. The sexy P.I. she hires as a bodyguard can do more than protect her—he just might end up saving her life.

Spencer Breck—London's father may have passed away, but he still throws a long shadow over Judd's past and London's future and may hold the key to both.

Jay Breck—London's uncle had a falling out with London's father. Could the rift between the brothers be the source of London's current turmoil?

Niles Breck—London's cousin has millions to his name, but his desire for more will get him in trouble.

Roger Taylor—He already helps London manage Breck Global Enterprises, but he wants more from her and may decide to take it.

Richard Taylor—He's been running Breck Global Enterprises for a long time; it's only natural he'd resent any interference from London.

Wade Vickers—London's half brother seems content with his role in his father's company, but does his cool exterior mask a raging jealousy?

Captain Williams—This SFPD detective knew both Judd's father and London's father, which means he knows all their secrets, but do they know his?

Chapter One

"Your father was murdered. You could be next."

London Breck jerked her head up from the slip of paper and caught the waiter's arm as he turned away. "I'm sorry. Who gave this to you?"

The young man's eyes widened and London released her death grip on his white jacket.

"Like I told you, Ms. Breck. I found the folded piece of paper on my tray with your name written on the outside. I—I don't know who put it there…and I didn't read it."

She crumpled the note in her fist and dropped it into her evening clutch, trading it for a ten-dollar bill. "That's okay. Thanks for delivering it to me."

The waiter pocketed the money and scurried away without looking back.

Someone had decided to play a joke with that note, or it signaled the opening gambit of some sort of scam. London tucked a stray strand of hair behind her ear. If this con man believed he could pull a fast one on her or Breck Global Enterprises, he hadn't met their legal team.

She straightened her spine and turned to face the room, smiling so hard her cheeks hurt. It was an occupational hazard—if one could call glad-handing and raising money an occupation. But it was the only one she'd ever had, the only one she'd ever trained for.

She swept a champagne flute from a passing tray with practiced ease and turned her attention to the crowd jamming the Fairmont Hotel's ballroom. Which well-heeled donor or wannabe had left that note? Scanning the room, her gaze tripped over the hottie in the corner.

Even though his crisp tux conformed to the dress code for the evening, he had *outsider* scribbled all over his amazing body. The tux couldn't mask the sheer power of the man, and it had very little to do with the way the material puckered and stretched across his massive shoulders, crying out for a good tailor.

His stance, his demeanor—okay, the dark sunglasses—marked him as a member of the bevy of body- and security guards that littered the room, jealously watching their clients or their clients' jewels or both. Probably not the author of the note, but definitely worth a closer inspection.

The note almost forgotten, London squinted at the pretty people bedecked in diamonds and designer duds and wondered which one had invited that powerful panther into the midst of the pampered trust-fund babies and oily politicians.

"Don't you know squinting like that will bring on the wrinkles, my dear?"

London rolled a sip of champagne on her tongue as she eyed her cousin. *Speaking of trust-fund babies...*

"Have you seen Roger tonight?"

"Your square-jawed, preppy suitor?" Niles shook his head. "For someone practically running the company, he sure misses a lot of soirees, doesn't he?"

She drew her fingertip around the rim of her glass. She didn't want to talk about the company. "Did you bid on something fabulous, Niles?"

"Of course I did. It's all rather too late, though, isn't it?" He plucked a cracker brimming with caviar from the tray on the table and studied it before popping it into his mouth.

"Too late?" She steadied herself for one of her cousin's acidic barbs.

He brushed his fingers together. "Here we are raising all this money for heart disease, but your father, Spencer Breck, already bit the dust, leaving you gazillions of dollars and handing you the reins of Breck Global. Should've had this fund-raiser *before* he kicked the bucket."

"I can always count on you to say the right thing at the right moment, bringing light and comfort."

Niles clicked his tongue, a decidedly feminine gesture she was sure Mr. Dark Sunglasses over in the corner had never made in his life.

Then Niles leaned in, his booze-soaked breath tickling her ear. "This is your cousin Niles. You don't have to pretend with me, my dear. I know you despised the man as much as I did."

He threw his silk scarf over his shoulder and waltzed away, throwing a kiss at a dowager across the room.

Maybe Niles had written that note to stir up trouble. She wouldn't put it past him. His own father had left Niles gazillions of dollars, but it was never enough for Niles.

Besides, Niles and his father, her late uncle Jay, might have despised Spencer, but her relationship with him had contained many more nuances than simple dislike.

She placed her champagne glass down next to the plate of caviar. The abrupt action caused the sparkling liquid to slosh over the rim. A waiter appeared as if by magic, whisking away the glass, replacing it with a fresh one and blotting the drops of champagne from the white tablecloth with a thick napkin. He even swapped out the plate of caviar, although none of the liquid had touched it.

The dull throbbing in her head from earlier in the evening made a repeat performance. She had to get away from the chatter.

She turned and collided with a brick wall—a brick wall

in a fine wool suit. The man with the sunglasses caught her arm with a surprisingly gentle grip.

"I'm sorry." His voice was a deep baritone that sent shocks of awareness up her spine.

He wasn't wearing sunglasses anymore and she stared into the bluest eyes she'd ever seen. "M-my fault."

He released her arm and strode past her.

She watched his broad back as he cut a swath through the partygoers. He landed in front of Bunny Harris and ducked as the older woman whispered something in his ear.

Watching the exchange, London sucked in her lower lip. Was he one of Bunny's escorts? If so, the old dame's taste in men had gone up several notches.

London slipped out of the room and headed for the ladies' restroom. On the way, Captain Williams from the San Francisco police department stopped her.

"This is a wonderful benefit, London. I'm sure your father would've been proud."

"Thank you, Captain."

He shook a finger in her face. "How many times do I have to tell you to call me Les? I've known you since you were a little girl, but you're a grown woman now. Les will do."

"I'll try to remember that…Les. If you'll excuse me." She'd been inching away from him during their conversation and was able to turn and make a break for it. If Captain Les Williams thought she had any pull to get him the chief's job, he'd better start kissing someone else's backside. Her father, with his connections to the SFPD, hadn't been able to do it, so she sure as hell couldn't.

She pushed through the ladies' room door. A couple of women were primping at the vanity and stopped their gossip long enough to smile at London in the mirror.

She nodded and swept past them to the restroom. Leaning against the tile counter, she dug into her clutch for an ibuprofen. She cupped some water in her hand from the faucet and swallowed the gelcap.

The voices of the women in the outer room rose and then a man burst through the bathroom door, holding his hand in front of him. "Don't be alarmed, Ms. Breck. I'd just like to ask you a few questions. Ray Lopez from KFGG. You might've seen my show."

She'd need to pop another ibuprofen at this rate. Instead she wedged a hand on her hip. "Really? You're following me into the ladies' room to get an interview?"

"Just a comment."

"You can't call my office?"

He spread his hands as he smiled. "You know and I know it's not that easy to reach you at your…office. Just a quick question about your father's death."

One of the women from the other room had followed the reporter into the bathroom and skewered him with an icy gaze. "Security is on the way."

He shrugged and stepped closer to London.

"I've already done that interview, Mr. Lopez—just not with you." She turned toward the mirror and ran the pad of her thumb over one eyebrow.

"You didn't answer this question. Did you find your father's death suspicious?"

"Not at all." She backed away from the mirror and tucked her bag under her arm, brushing past Lopez. Had he written the threatening note to manufacture some story? Why would he ask that question? She wouldn't give him the satisfaction of asking him about his motives.

As she took one step out of the lounge, a security guard barreled past her. "Sir, you're not allowed in the ladies' room. I'm going to have to escort you out of the hotel."

Lopez craned his head over his shoulder to give her one last look as the security guard hustled him toward the escalator.

She blew out a long breath. She couldn't even escape notice in the ladies' bathroom. She'd had enough, enough of the pretense and the fake smiles and the eager reporters... and the vaguely threatening notes. Her father had passed away just last month—of natural causes. Surely she could be excused for having a headache and leaving the shindig early.

She plucked her phone from her purse and called her driver. "Theodore, I'm ready to go. Meet me in the side alley. I don't want to go through the front entrance."

"Paparazzi stalking you again, Ms. Breck?"

"You have no idea."

"On my way."

When she entered the ballroom, she located her cousin, who was telling some risqué story and taking liberties with the truth. She crooked her finger at him and he broke away from his adoring audience.

"I'm getting out of here. People already think I was terribly brave making an appearance so soon after Dad's death."

"Especially since he did go off rather abruptly."

Was everyone drinking the same water? Lifting her shoulders, she said, "He *did* have heart disease."

"Although all his money allowed him to manage it quite well."

"Did you send me a note tonight, Niles?"

"A note?" His tweezed eyebrows shot to his hairline. "What are you talking about?"

"Nothing. Never mind." Had she really expected him to confess? Of course, maybe she'd just put him on notice.

She flicked her fingers at the room, still buzzing with activity. "Could you please do the honors for me? Announce the winners of the silent auction, thank everyone for coming and so on and son on."

He patted her arm with his long, thin hand. "I'd be happy

to, my dear. You go home and get a good night's sleep and dream of your billions."

She sighed. "You're not exactly in the poorhouse, cousin."

"Ah, but your father was the lucky one—and the greedy one."

"I already have a headache. Let's not get into family politics." She kissed the air somewhere near his cheek and pivoted on her heel.

She nearly bumped into Bunny Harris at the coat check, hanging on to a much younger man's arm, but not the man with the sunglasses. "So sorry, Bunny. Are you off already?"

"Don't worry, London. I made a sizable donation to the cause. Your father was one of my oldest friends. I'll miss him."

"Thank you." London's gaze strayed over Bunny's shoulder to her model-handsome companion lounging against the coat-check window.

Bunny slid her ticket across the counter with one manicured fingertip. "Oh, this is…"

"Lance." The man reached around Bunny, extending his hand. "Ms. Breck."

"Nice to meet you." She shook his hand and then dropped it. "Enjoy the rest of your evening."

Lance draped Bunny's fur around her shoulders and they descended the escalator to the lobby of the hotel.

Shaking her head, London dipped her hand into her purse for the claim ticket and felt the note. She pulled it out with the ticket and examined the block letters written with a black felt-tip pen.

She'd hold on to it for a day or two in case there was a follow-up and then turn it over to Breck Global's security team. It could very well be that reporter trying some angle.

The coat-check clerk plopped her leather bomber jacket on the counter. "Cool jacket."

London smiled, handed her a tip and headed for the escalator, hugging the jacket to her chest. When she hit the first step, she gathered the skirt of her long dress in one hand and lifted it.

She glided into the lobby and a bellhop sprang to life. "Do you need a taxi, Ms. Breck?"

"No, thanks. My driver's waiting." Technically, Theodore was her father's driver, but she didn't have the heart to let him go, even though she felt silly with a driver.

She stuffed her arms into her jacket and pulled out her phone to check the time. If Theodore had taken the car back to her father's Pacific Heights mansion, it shouldn't take him more than ten or fifteen minutes to get here.

She parked herself in front of a rack of flyers and studied the trips to Alcatraz and the wine country for a few minutes. Then she glanced over her shoulder at a few people crisscrossing the lobby. No photographers, no Ray Lopez, although they could be waiting for her out front. She pushed through the side door of the hotel. Lifting her skirts, she traipsed down the steps and shoved open the heavy metal door to the outside.

It slammed behind her.

The dark alley glistened with moisture. Theodore hadn't made it yet. She squinted toward the street, partially blocked by a Dumpster.

He must've taken the car somewhere else on his break. She turned toward the side door and grabbed the handle, pressing it down. The door didn't budge.

A footstep crunched behind her, but before she had time to turn around, an arm hooked around her throat.

She should've braved the paparazzi.

Chapter Two

Locked in a stall in the men's room, Judd slipped the velvet pouch crammed with jewels into the inside pocket of his dinner jacket. He patted his .45 tucked into the shoulder holster on the other side.

He had no idea where Bunny Harris would wind up with that gigolo she'd picked up tonight, but at least her jewelry wouldn't be with her.

He shoved out of the stall and nodded at the man washing his hands at the vanity, who'd caught his eye in the mirror. The dude had been talking to London Breck earlier—probably a relative. As far as he knew, the richest woman in the city didn't have a husband or even a boyfriend. The tabloids linked her with a new man every other month… not that he followed the tabloids except for business.

The man at the sink and London had the same look—blond, Nordic, cold. Although London was a beautiful girl, she wasn't his type, even with all those dollar signs after her name.

Judd washed his hands, accepted a warm towel from the attendant and slipped a five in his basket. He turned toward the door.

"Care for a spritz?"

Judd stumbled to a stop and glanced over his shoulder at the mirror.

The Breck relative held up a bottle of cologne, aiming it at him. "It's a good scent…manly."

"That's okay." Judd held up his hands. "I'm good."

He heard the hiss of the spray bottle behind him as he dodged through the bathroom door. *Rich people.*

Checking his watch, he jogged down the escalator. Bunny had told him she'd send her car back for him at the side entrance to the hotel. He waved to the hotel clerk and gave a fist bump to one of the bellhops.

"Later, man."

He took the steps down to the side door two at a time and pushed through to the alley. Darkness enveloped him as his shoes crunched broken glass. He tilted back his head to look at the lights on the outside of the hotel, which had been smashed.

His head jerked up at the sound of scuffling down the alley, and he noticed a car parked at the end, blocking the entrance to the street, contributing to the darkness.

He plucked a small but powerful flashlight from his pocket and aimed it in the direction of the noise.

A man wearing a ski mask looked up from the woman he was dragging behind him by the throat.

"Hey!" Judd sprinted toward the scene.

The man dropped his victim and rushed to the waiting car at the end of the alley. Tires squealed and the car peeled out before Judd could reach it. He flicked his light at the retreating vehicle, but someone had removed the back license plate.

A woman coughed behind him and he spun around and strode back to her. The sparkly material of her gown was twisted around her legs and she couldn't stand. He scooped her up and set her on her impossibly high heels. No wonder she couldn't run away from her assailant.

She brushed strands of blond hair from her face. That silvery hair seemed to be the only source of light in the alley—that and the sparkles on her black dress and at her throat.

She coughed again, swore like a sailor and spit onto the concrete. "My God, if he wanted the necklace, why didn't he just ask?"

Judd found himself looking into the perfect face of London Breck, a little disheveled and mad as hell, but those qualities only seemed to enhance her beauty.

Her eyes widened and sparkled, matching the diamonds around her neck in brilliance. "You!"

"What the hell are you doing out here in the alley?" He bent over and swept her handbag from the ground. Odd the thief hadn't snatched that.

She grabbed it from him and folded her arms over her body. "Waiting for my driver. You?"

"Waiting for Bunny Harris's driver."

She swayed toward him and he caught her before she toppled over. She smelled…expensive, except for the odor of leather coming from her jacket. Who wore a jacket like that with a haute couture evening dress?

"Whoa." He pointed to her feet. "If you hope to stand upright on your own, you'd better straighten out that dress."

"I hate long dresses." She leaned forward and placed her hands on either side of a hole in her dress below her knees and pulled it apart.

The bottom part of her dress, which seemed to be made of different material from the top, ripped off, and she dropped the silky material, which probably cost more than his motorcycle, into a puddle in the alley.

"There." She thrust out her hand. "London Breck. Thanks for saving me from whatever that was."

"Judd Brody." He clasped her long, slim fingers in his hand, but if he expected a limp, girly handshake from her, he was wrong. She gave his hand a firm squeeze and dropped it.

"That was a robbery, wasn't it?" His gaze shifted to the bright bauble stuck on her right ring finger and the diamond bracelet now peeking from the cuff of the jacket.

She trailed her fingers across her throat. "At first I thought he wanted my necklace, but he was using it to choke me and drag me. He was pulling me to that waiting car."

"A kidnapping?" He lifted one eyebrow. "I suppose you're worth a few bucks."

She snorted. "Yeah, good luck with that. My cousin wouldn't pay one dime for my release, and I'm sure my board of directors would be happy to get rid of me."

A black limo pulled into the alley, bathing it in bright light. Judd cupped a hand over his eyes and squinted.

The car door swung open and a massive figure rolled from the car. "Miss Breck? Are you all right? I'm sorry I'm late. I had a little mishap on the way over."

She waved. "I'm fine, Theodore. Mr. Brody here rescued me from a would-be robber."

"What?" Theodore waddled toward them. "I told you not to be waiting in this alley."

"I expected you to be right here to whisk me away." She patted the big man's arm. "Not that I blame you, Theodore. Sh—stuff happens."

Theodore grabbed Judd's hand and shook his arm as if he wanted to yank it off. "Thank you, sir."

Another limo pulled into the alley and honked.

"Now, who is that?" Theodore tugged his cap over his eyes to shield out his headlights.

"I believe that's Ms. Harris's driver for me." Judd straightened his jacket and patted the hidden jewels.

Theodore tilted his head at him. "You one of Bunny's young men?"

London coughed and clapped a hand over her mouth. As long as Theodore had been working for the upper crust of the city, he'd never learned to filter his speech. She liked that.

"God, no. I'm working for her tonight…as a bodyguard."

"Can I buy you a drink?" London sniffed and ran her hand beneath her nose. "It's the least I can do. Theodore can take us."

"That I can," her driver added.

A drink with the rich and beautiful London Breck? Why not? Another way to make his older brothers jealous.

"Sure."

"I'll go tell Bunny's driver. I know him." Theodore turned and made his way down the alley, momentarily blocking out the headlights and casting him into darkness again with London.

She suddenly looked vulnerable with her silvery-blond hair half-down on one side and her ripped couture dress.

Judd tapped his neck. "Are you okay?"

"Throat's a little rough, but I'll live."

"Do you want to report it to the cops?"

"Did you get a license plate or a good look at the driver or my attacker?"

"The car didn't have a license plate and the driver was wearing a ski mask just like your assailant's, except for the white zigzag down the front."

"Then, no. I don't need the publicity."

Theodore shifted his formidable presence to the side and the headlights lit up the alley again. The beams picked up London's sparkles—her hair, her jewels, her dress—and she blazed to life. How had he ever imagined this woman had one vulnerable bone in her body?

"You get a lot of that, don't you? Publicity, I mean."

Spreading her hands, she shrugged. "Comes with the territory."

Theodore called from behind her, "I sent Mrs. Harris's driver away. Are you ready, Miss Breck?"

"After the night I just had? You bet."

She spun around on her high heels and picked her way through the puddles in the alley to the waiting town car.

Judd's gaze locked onto her swaying hips in the glittering material below the bomber jacket and the endless legs below the jagged hem of the skirt. London had a tall, slim build, but he wouldn't call her skinny.

Wouldn't kick her out of bed, either.

He motioned for the driver to get in the car first and held open the door as Theodore squeezed behind the wheel. Judd slammed the door after Theodore and ducked into the backseat.

It smelled like brand-new leather, which felt as smooth as butter beneath his fingertips as he adjusted himself on the seat next to London.

The glass between the front and backseats slid open. "Where to, Miss Breck?"

"How about Sneaky Pete's in the Lower Haight?"

"I don't think it's very safe down there, Miss Breck."

"I'm going to be with Bunny Harris's bodyguard, and he's—" she patted his chest "—packing heat."

"It's that obvious?"

"To the practiced eye." With her hand still on his chest, she ran those practiced eyes down to his thighs and a slow heat simmered his blood.

"And here I thought we were headed someplace upscale and trendy."

"I just want a quiet drink. Disappointed?" She snatched her hand back and dropped it into her lap where her ripped dress had ridden up, exposing her creamy thighs.

"Doesn't make any difference to me, but if we're headed that way, I need to make a stop first. Is that a problem?"

"Not for me." She leaned forward in her seat. "Theodore?"

"Not a problem, sir. Where to?"

Judd pulled the bag of jewels from his pocket and tossed

it on the seat between him and London. "I need to make a deposit at Bunny's house."

"I know exactly where the Harris house is. It's not too far from Mr. Breck's residence. We'll be there in less than fifteen minutes." The privacy glass magically slid into place while Theodore backed the car out of the alley and rolled onto the street.

"I'm sure this was your idea." London caressed the velvet pouch. "Bunny is notoriously careless, especially when she's met a new young stud."

"I noticed."

"Do you guard her body or her possessions?"

"This is a one-night gig for me. I was helping out a buddy, and the directive was to watch the jewels. When it was clear she'd made plans after the gala with someone she'd just met, I insisted she leave her jewels with me."

"You're one of *those* Brodys, aren't you?"

Why wouldn't she know his family? Hers had been in this city longer than his. He hunched forward and inspected the mobile liquor cabinet in front of him. "Yep."

"Congratulations."

"For what?" He lifted the lid from a cut-glass decanter half-full of dark amber liquid and sniffed the rich aroma.

"After all these years, it looks as though your brother and that true-crime writer uncovered the truth that your father wasn't the Phone Book Killer."

"I guess so." He investigated another decanter.

"You seem rather nonchalant about it all."

"Happened a long time ago." And he'd sealed off that part of his life in a cold little box in one corner of his heart. He'd let his older brothers gnash their teeth over the stain on the family name. He'd schooled himself not to think about it…or his father.

Her hand covered his, grasping the decanter. "Do you want a drink?"

That smooth skin against his did things to his insides. Was she that smooth all over? That perfect? He'd have fun getting her a little dirty.

His gaze wandered to the tinted glass. Would Theodore mind? This backseat afforded plenty of room to twist this leggy blonde into a pretzel. But she deserved more than a quickie.

He stared into her murky green eyes. "I can wait."

As her hand left his, she trailed her short, polished fingernails across his skin and he suppressed a shiver.

This one might be made of ice, but she liked to play with fire. He'd seen the tabloids—London Breck jumping naked into a fountain, London Breck running away from home at seventeen to join a rock band on tour, London Breck getting arrested in Qatar for having one of the world's largest diamonds in her possession, which she'd claimed a married sheikh had given her.

Slumming it with a lowly P.I. could be her next crazy prank.

Hell, he was game.

What made him think she wasn't his type? Any gorgeous woman who was up for a good time was his type.

The car slid to a smooth stop at the gates of a mansion in Pacific Heights. The city lights created a twinkling river before them.

The intercom clicked on and Theodore's voice rumbled across the speaker. "I don't know if we can get past the security gates, sir."

"Mrs. Harris and I made arrangements. Pull up to the call box, Theodore."

The car turned into the driveway and stopped at the intercom at the gate. Judd punched the button and held it in.

"Hello?"

"This is Judd Brody."

"Of course, Mr. Brody. Mrs. Harris left instructions."

The gate eased open and Theodore drove the car around the short, circular drive in front of the Victorian mansion. Did London live in a place like this up here?

"I'll be right back." Judd swung open the door before Theodore could get out and open it for him. He strode up the front porch and rang the doorbell, which chimed somewhere deep in the house.

The door opened a crack and an eyeball assessed him. Then the crack widened and the pinched face of Bunny's butler appeared.

Judd held out the pouch. "Mrs. Harris wants these to go right back in the safe."

"Yes, of course." The butler snatched the pouch with long, bony fingers and pressed it to his heart. "Thank you, Mr. Brody, for looking after Bunny's treasures."

"I think someone else is looking after her treasures now."

He left the butler standing at the door with his mouth gaping open, launched off the porch and grabbed the handle of the car door.

He fell onto the seat and ran a hand through his hair. "On to Sneaky Pete's."

The car lurched forward and London fell against his shoulder. She took her time getting back into her own space. So she felt it, too?

He'd better maintain control. The drive to the Haight wasn't that long—not nearly long enough for what he planned for London.

He cleared his throat. "Do you live in Pacific Heights?"

"No." She shook her head and her hair shimmered. "I live on Nob Hill, but my father has a place here. I'm not moving."

He shot a quick glance at her luscious lips, now pressed

into a determined line. His simple question had changed the mood in the car.

London kept her hands in her lap and stared out the window. She seemed to have lost interest in their flirtation, so maybe he wouldn't be getting lucky with an heiress tonight.

Theodore pulled the car to the curb, but this time Judd didn't beat him to the door. Theodore opened London's door with a wrinkled brow beneath his cap. "I don't like this, Miss Breck."

"It's all good, Theodore. Do you want to join us for a drink?"

He crossed his arms, resting them on his big belly. "I don't drink and drive. Never have, never will."

Judd clambered from the car and eyed the seedy bar with the psychedelic mural on the outside wall and a flickering red neon sign. "I'll take care of her, Theodore."

"Thank you, sir."

London heaved an exaggerated sigh, but she didn't protest. "You can take the car home, Theodore. We can get a taxi later."

"I have my own code. I take you somewhere, and I bring you back. Call when you're ready."

"If you insist." She winked at Judd.

"Hold on." Judd shed his dinner jacket, shrugged out of his cummerbund and pulled off his bow tie. He tossed them into the backseat of the car. "I don't want to be overdressed."

London tugged her motorcycle jacket closed over the sparkly material of her dress. "You have a point."

Judd opened the door of the bar and ushered her through. The neon motif from outside carried forward to the interior. Standard-issue neon beer signs flashed on the walls, and a jukebox in the corner cranked out a hard-rock tune. If smoking in bars were allowed in this city, this would be a smoke-filled room.

Instead patrons cracked peanut shells and dropped them on the floor as they gathered around tables or hunched over the bar. A few couples danced on the wood floor of a small room off the main bar. Nobody looked at them twice.

Rolling up the sleeves of his white shirt, Judd led London to a table near the jukebox and slid onto the wood bench across from her. "Come here often?"

"Every once in a while." Her gaze scanned the tattoos spilling down one of his arms, and she pointed to the long bar of scarred wood. "We can order at the bar. The waitresses here are few and far between."

"I'm in no hurry, are you?" He caught the eye of a waitress in a pair of short shorts and a tie-dyed T-shirt tied under her breasts.

She scurried over, balancing a tray of drinks with one hand. "What can I get you?"

"I'll have a beer, whatever you have on tap."

"I'll take the same." London turned wide eyes on him. "How did you get her to come over here so fast?"

He shrugged. "I just made eye contact. It works better than yelling."

Her gaze dropped from his face and meandered across his chest, where he'd undone the first few buttons of his shirt. His flesh warmed in the wake of her inventory.

"Yeah, whatever." She folded her arms on the table. "So what do you normally do for a living when you're not helping out friends guarding jewels for rich, frisky matrons?"

"Guard jewels for rich, frisky matrons."

"Really?"

He stretched his legs out to the side of the table. "I'm a private investigator and bodyguard. Usually my assignments are more long-term than this one. I just got back from a job in Saudi Arabia."

"I know a few people in that part of the world." She flashed her teeth in more of a grimace than a smile and drummed her fingernails on the table. "Is it interesting work?"

"It can be. There's a lot of travel involved, which I like."

"I like to travel, too." She stopped fidgeting and pressed her palms together. "Things will be a little different for me now, now that…"

"Your father died. Sorry for your loss."

"Thank you."

"He left you in charge?"

Her eyes narrowed and glittered. "You sound surprised."

"You sound defensive."

She puffed out a breath, blowing a strand of hair from her eyes. "Let's just say I'm dealing with a lot right now. Lots of unhappy people never expected Dad to put the reins of Breck Global Enterprises in the hands of his flighty daughter."

"You're his only child?" He knew that, of course, even if he didn't follow San Francisco society closely, except when he needed to for his clients. But he stubbornly wanted to pretend he knew nothing about her famous family.

"Only legitimate one." She rubbed her chin. "I do have a half brother. I'm sure my father would've preferred me as the bastard and Wade as the legitimate son. You have three brothers, right?"

He raised his brows but held his response as the waitress delivered their drinks and a bowl of peanuts.

The waitress asked, "Do you want anything to eat?"

"No, thanks." He tipped his chin at London. "You?"

"Not after all that rich food at the benefit."

He sipped the dark, malty beer through the thick head of foam and met London's purposeful look over the rim of the glass.

"Three brothers? I know one's a cop in the city, and then there's the one who was working with that writer."

"You seem to know a lot about my family."

"The Brody family is in the news almost as much as my family." Her lips puckered and she blew on the foam in her glass.

"For very different reasons." He shifted his gaze away from that kissable mouth. He'd let her make all the moves.

"While you're all busy delivering justice, the Brecks are delivering…money."

"Both equally necessary. Besides, I don't deliver justice. I just look out for pretty people and their pretty things."

He didn't believe in justice—not after losing his father when he was practically a baby and then his mother to drugs and alcohol. Sean had been a great big brother, but a sibling was no substitute for a mom and dad.

"Thank God for that." London clinked her mug with his.

The song on the jukebox had changed to a slow ballad all about how love hurt, and Judd took a swig of beer. Hell, love didn't hurt, not if you dropped it in its tracks.

London rapped her knuckles on the table between them. "You wanna dance?"

"You're kidding."

"There are some couples out there." She jerked her thumb over her shoulder at the postage-stamp dance floor.

"That doesn't mean we have to join them."

She tugged on his rolled-up sleeve. "Come on. I promise not to jump on the tabletop."

Her cool fingers brushed against his skin, causing a thudding ache in the middle of his belly. "Have you been known to do that? Jump on tabletops?"

Her fingernails dug into his forearm. "Don't pretend you don't know about me, Judd Brody."

Busted. He jumped from the booth. If this was some weird mating ritual she had, he'd play along.

When they hit the dance floor, he pulled her snug against his body. Who did she think she was toying with, some upper-crust rich boy? He didn't play games. If a woman signaled interest the way London was doing, he'd take her up on the offer every time.

Wrapping one arm around her slender waist, he reached up with his other hand to tuck her head against his shoulder. Her breath warmed his skin through the thin material of his shirt.

He rested his cheek against her bright hair, and the golden strands stuck to the stubble of his beard. Reaching between their bodies, he opened her leather jacket and drew her close, his chest pressing against her soft breasts beneath the silvery material of her dress.

She shifted and her soft lips touched the side of his neck.

He gritted his teeth to suppress the shudder threatening to engulf his body. Her expensive perfume enveloped them, and for the first time in a very long time and a very long line of women, he felt on the edge of losing control.

Then the door to the bar burst open and Theodore, bloodied and battered, staggered into the room and dropped to the floor.

Chapter Three

London screamed at the bloody mess that was Theodore's face and twisted out of the comfort of Judd's embrace, pitching forward. Judd curled one muscular arm around her waist to steady her.

He tucked her behind his large frame and strode toward Theodore, who had collapsed in a heap.

She made a grab for Judd's belt and hooked two fingers through the loop, following him as people cleared a path to Theodore's inert form.

Judd yelled over his shoulder at the bartender, "Call nine-one-one. Now!"

He crouched beside Theodore, feeling for his pulse. "Towels, I need some clean towels to stop this bleeding."

"I-is he still alive? Has he been shot?" London had never seen so much blood. She unbuttoned Theodore's shirt at the neck.

"He's still breathing, and I don't see any bullet wounds."

The waitress who had served them earlier rushed from behind the bar with a stack of white towels. "Is he okay?"

"He's lost consciousness."

One of the bartenders knelt beside Judd with a pitcher of water. "Ambulance is on the way. Do you need this?"

London dipped one of the towels in the water and dabbed

Theodore's split lip as Judd pressed another against the gaping wound on his head.

Taking Theodore's big hand in hers, London squeezed it and whispered, "You're going to be okay."

The wailing sirens scattered the crowd of people hovering over Theodore. When the EMTs rushed in, Judd talked to them as they worked on their patient.

Once the EMTs bundled Theodore into the ambulance, a police officer approached Judd. "Do you know the victim?"

Judd turned to London. "He's her driver."

"Black limo? License number—" the officer flipped open a notepad "—BGE21?"

London's heart fluttered in her chest. "That's right. What happened to Theodore? Where's the car?"

The officer tapped the pad of paper against his chin. "The car's registered to Spencer Breck and Breck Global Enterprises."

"That's me." London waved her hand. "I'm Breck Global Enterprises."

The cop's eyes widened for a second and then shifted to the diamond necklace around her throat. "Of course, Ms. Breck. The car—your car—was found idling at the curb by the park. The driver's-side door was open and it looks as if the car had rolled partially into the street and then was hit by another car."

Judd's head shot up. "Was there blood near the car? On the seat?"

"Exactly. It appears that someone pulled the driver from the car and beat him on the street. His plans to steal the car were probably thwarted when it rolled into the street and got hit." The officer's eyebrows met over his nose. "And you are?"

"Judd Brody."

"Brody…"

"He's my friend. Is that what you think this was? An attempted car theft? Of a limo?"

"Could've been kids looking for a joyride." He scratched his chin and eyed Judd. "Aren't you...?"

Judd sliced his hand through the air. "I don't think kids could've done that much damage to a big guy like Theodore."

Good to know she and Judd were on the same page. Wedging her hand on her hip, she said, "I don't think kids would be out to steal a distinctive limo, either."

"That might be just what they wanted. We don't have any witnesses. I'm amazed your driver made it this far in his condition. He should've just called the cops himself."

The officer asked them several more questions and told her where the ambulance had transported Theodore. He had a daughter in New York and one in Atlanta, and she intended to call both of them just as soon as she checked up on Theodore herself.

How could this happen? Theodore had never run into any trouble driving her father around. She couldn't even keep her employees safe. How was she supposed to run a company? Maybe she did need Roger's help.

She arranged for a tow service to take the limo back to her father's place, and Judd called a taxi.

London twisted her fingers into knots. "It's all my fault. I should've insisted that he take the car back instead of waiting around in this crappy neighborhood."

"The only people who deserve blame are the dirtbags who tried to jack Theodore." He brushed a wisp of hair from her cheek with the rough pad of his finger. "There's no way you were going to convince Theodore to leave you. He takes pride in a job well done."

"You're right, but we should've gone somewhere else." She shoved her hands in the pockets of her jacket. "I need to stop being the wild-child free spirit."

He wedged a finger beneath her chin and tilted her head back. "Who says?"

His soft touch and low voice caused tears to prick the backs of her eyes. How had he gone from sexy alpha male on the dance floor to this man with the understanding eyes? And why was she falling under his spell so quickly?

She jerked her head away and ducked to peer through the window. "I think our taxi's here."

They climbed into the backseat and she put her hand on his forearm, which tensed beneath her fingers. "Your jacket's in the back of the limo."

"Don't worry about it. I don't think I'll be needing it anytime soon."

"Where do you live?" She leaned forward in her seat.

"We'll have him drop you off first."

She gave the taxi driver her address and fell back against the seat. "I hope Theodore's going to be okay. Maybe we should follow the ambulance."

"And have you create a media circus? Not a great idea. Theodore lost a lot of blood, but I've seen guys a lot worse off than that after fights. I think he'll pull through."

"Thanks to you. Is all that first aid—" she waved her hand in the air "—part of your job?"

"Yeah. I spent several summers working as a lifeguard in Santa Cruz, so I had all that training, which comes in handy now."

She closed her eyes. Was there anything this man couldn't do?

Too quickly, the taxi pulled in front of her building.

Judd tapped the driver's shoulder. "Wait here. I'll be right back."

He took her hand to help her from the car and dropped it all too soon as they walked to the front door of her building. She entered the code to open the door and turned on the step. Under better circumstances she'd invite him up for a cocktail, see if his slow seduction on the dance floor would come to fruition.

Now she just wanted to wash her hands, still smudged with Theodore's blood.

"Thanks for everything tonight, Judd Brody."

"You're welcome, London Breck. Do you need me to walk you up to your place?"

She pointed inside the lobby at the security guard sitting at the desk watching TV monitors. "Twenty-four-hour security here. I'm not the only celebrity in the building."

"Good, but don't forget how the evening started, with you being attacked in an alley."

Judd didn't even know about the threatening note. "I guess Theodore and I both had targets on our backs tonight."

His brow furrowed. "Yeah, you did."

He obviously wasn't going to sweep her into his arms for a good-night kiss, no matter how much she needed the comfort, so she stuck out her hand. "Good night."

"Goodbye." He gave her hand a hard squeeze and then turned away.

Ouch. That had a ring of finality to it. Why shouldn't it? They were two strangers thrown together by two extraordinary events. They'd shared a little flirtation, but so what? A man like Judd Brody must have had many little flirtations to his credit…and many notches on his bedpost.

She had more important matters to think about anyway. She waved to the security guard as she crossed the marble-tiled lobby. She had to grow up and take charge of a multibillion-dollar enterprise—and Judd Brody couldn't help with that at all.

THE FOLLOWING DAY, London scooted the plastic chair closer to the bed and patted Theodore's arm. "I don't get why someone would want to carjack a limousine. And why did you go to the bar instead of calling the police?"

Theodore moved his head from side to side and groaned.

"Keep still." She reached for the plastic cup on the table beside his hospital bed and held the straw to his swollen lips.

He sipped some water and then waved it away. "Pulled me out of the car, and I lost my phone in the fight. I wouldn't let them…wouldn't let them take the car."

"That's just silly. Why are you protecting a heap of metal? You should've let them have the damn thing and saved yourself."

"Couldn't let them. Had to protect you."

"Me?" She folded the sheet under his side. "I wasn't even there. I was perfectly safe at the bar with—at the bar."

She'd fallen asleep thinking about Judd's arms wrapped around her on the dance floor, about the way the warm skin of his throat felt against her lips. Then she heard his goodbye. Curt. Final.

"If they got the car…they could get you."

Her gaze darted to his face and she flashed on the threatening note from last night. "What does that mean?"

But Theodore had closed his eyes, and his breathing deepened.

His nurse bustled into the room. "Is he sleeping? I gave him something for the pain."

"How much longer will he be here?"

"You'll have to ask him. You're not next of kin, and we can't reveal those details."

London rolled her eyes and rose from the chair. "His medical expenses are covered by an insurance policy with Breck Global. I have his medical card."

"If you can drop that off at the nurses' station, they'll take care of getting that to billing."

Ten minutes later, London retrieved her Mini from the

hospital's subterranean parking garage and decided to check out the limo, which the tow truck had brought to her father's place. Why had Theodore thought he was protecting her by not allowing the carjackers to take the car? Maybe he hadn't wanted them to get the keys or the car registration, but the registration listed the address of BGE, not her place in Nob Hill.

She maneuvered through the traffic on Van Ness and turned toward Lafayette Park, rolling through the well-ordered streets with their manicured lawns. The tow-truck driver must've used the remote control in the limo for the gate, because he'd parked the car in the driveway.

London opened the front gate to the mansion with her key. The couple who looked after the house was still living here. London didn't have the heart to turn them out any more than she could let Theodore go.

The limo sported a dent in the left front panel and a smashed window. The cops had tried to lift prints from the vehicle, but hadn't had any luck.

She opened the door and shivered at the sight of Theodore's blood on the leather seat. She'd get the car detailed at the same time she dropped it off for bodywork. Peering under the seats, she spotted Theodore's cell phone and pulled it out.

He had left the sliding partition between the front and back seats open and a heap of material caught her eye—Judd's dinner jacket. A thrill of excitement zipped up her spine. Now she had an excuse to call him. Then she remembered his abrupt goodbye. Victor at the house could earn his salary by returning Judd's jacket to him.

Grabbing the handle of the back door, she yanked it open. She fell across the seat and buried her face in the fine material of Judd's jacket, inhaling the masculine scent that clung to its folds.

"Ms. Breck?"

She recognized Anna, the housekeeper's, voice, and rolled to her back, hunching up on her elbows. "Hello, Anna."

"Are you okay?"

Anna's lips twitched with disapproval and London knew whatever response she made, Anna would never think she was okay. Anna had been around since before her mother died, had been around for all the craziness and the acting out and…all the other stuff.

"I'm fine. Victor told you what happened to Theodore, didn't he?"

"Foolish man." Her nostrils flared. "He should've let them have the car."

"That's what I told him, but he said he was protecting me."

Anna's face puckered as if she'd just sucked a lemon. "Are you going to get the car fixed?"

"Yes, I was just—" She plucked at Judd's jacket. "My friend left his jacket in the car."

Anna screwed her face up even more, leaving no doubt about what she thought London and her so-called friend had been doing in the backseat of the limo.

She should've been so lucky.

"Maybe Victor can return it to him."

"Of course. Are you staying, Ms. Breck?"

"No. I just wanted to get my friend's stuff." *And roll around in it while I think of his hard body.*

The old London would've voiced those exact words just to see Anna's face implode, but the new London, the CEO London, kept those thoughts to herself.

"You can give your friend's items and an address to Victor. He'll be happy to return them." Anna's rubber-soled shoes squelched on the damp flagstones as she went back to the house.

When London heard the front door shut, she collapsed

against the seat again, against Judd's jacket, her arm dangling to the floor of the car. Her fingers met the stiff cummerbund Judd had discarded and something else—something soft and fuzzy.

She closed her hand around it and held it above her face. She drew her brows together. It was a beanie, a watch cap. No, a ski mask.

A ski mask with a white zigzag down the front.

Chapter Four

Judd tossed his cell phone onto the desk and leaned back in his secondhand chair, which squeaked in protest. He wanted to find out how Theodore was doing, but he couldn't get anything out of the hospital and he didn't have any pull with the SFPD with his brother Sean still on a leave of absence.

He watched the pedestrians in the street from his small second-story office in North Beach. He had only one room with an old desk, two chairs, a bookshelf and a dying plant, but it kept his clients away from his apartment.

Yawning, he scratched the stubble on his chin. He'd had a cancellation and should be using the downtime to do some paperwork, but he hated paperwork. He needed an admin assistant, but didn't like people poking around his business, and there wasn't enough room in this office for a second person.

He grabbed his phone again and traced the edges with his fingertip. It would be easy enough to leave a message for London at the BGE offices. She did still have his dinner jacket from last night. He could use that as an excuse.

Smacking the phone against his palm, he swore. Why did he need an excuse? She wasn't the queen. He could call her if he wanted to call her.

He dropped the cell on his desk again. He knew damned well her wealth and power weren't deterring him from contacting her. It was the way she made him feel—and those feelings had *danger* written all over them.

He ran a hand through his hair. "Let it go, Brody."

"Let what go?"

He stared at the vision outlined by the open door of his office as if he'd conjured her from his mind. London had one hand on her hip and the other supporting her on the doorjamb. Faded denim encased her long legs and a pair of high-heeled boots hit just above her knee. A green sweater with a dipping neckline matched her eyes, and she'd pulled her silvery-blond hair into a ponytail that fell over one shoulder.

Danger.

"How'd you find me?"

"You're kidding, right?" She launched into the room, sweeping a bag from the floor on her way in. "I have BGE's formidable resources at the tips of my fingers."

"How's Theodore doing?"

"He's out of danger. I called his daughters this morning, and one is coming out in a few days."

"That's good."

Dropping the bag at her feet, London scanned the room. "This sort of reminds me of Philip Marlowe's office."

"Um, I don't have any palm trees swaying in the Santa Ana winds out my window."

She spun around, arms flung out to her sides. "You know what I mean—cramped quarters, battered old desk, piles of paper all over."

"You make it sound so…charming." He pointed to the bag on the floor. "Are those the rest of my clothes?"

"Yes." She folded her hands in front of her, an expectant look on her face.

She must've wanted to see him, or she would've sent one of her lackeys over here. Did she want him to ask her out? Continue their game of flirtation? Take her across his battered old desk?

He cleared his throat and wedged one motorcycle boot against the edge of the desk—just in case.

"I—I have a proposition for you."

A pulse thudded in his throat. He liked propositions from beautiful women. He could sweep all this junk off his desk in two seconds. "Yeah?"

"I want to…hire you."

He crashed to earth but kept his expression immobile. "To do what?"

"To do what you do." She flicked her fingers in the air. "To be my bodyguard."

He clenched his jaw. Bad idea. Instead of dating him, did she think she could keep him on a chain, yanking him this way and that, barking orders? He didn't roll that way.

"No." He let his foot drop heavily to the floor.

She blinked and then widened her eyes. "Why not? That's your profession, isn't it? If it's the money—"

He held up a hand. "I know you're good for it, but I don't do that type of bodyguarding."

"What type?" She tilted her head and her ponytail swung to the other shoulder.

"The general you-can-be-my-lapdog-and-carry-my-shopping-bags type." He pushed to his feet and folded his arms across his chest, flexing just in case she didn't get the message.

Her lips parted and a rosy flush spread across her cheeks. "I'm not—you're not—it's not like that."

"Really."

"I need a protector, not a lapdog." She reached into the bag, pulled out his dinner jacket and tossed it onto the desk. She threw the cummerbund over her shoulder onto the floor. Then she straightened to her full height, plus five-inch heels, clutching a black watch cap to her chest.

"I need protection from this." Pinching the cap between two fingers, she dangled it in front of him.

His eyes narrowed as he took in the ski mask with the white lightning bolt down the front of it. "Where'd you find that?"

"It was in the backseat of the limo." She jiggled it so that it danced between them. "One of the carjackers, because Theodore confirmed there were two, must've lost it in the struggle. The same ski mask he wore when he attacked me outside the hotel last night."

"Let me see it." He held out his hand and she dropped it onto his palm. He stretched it out and traced the white pattern. "It's definitely the same one."

"Someone attacked me last night and then followed the limo and for whatever reason tried to steal it from Theodore."

"Sure looks that way." He poked his fingers into the eyeholes of the mask. "Maybe he got a good look at your diamonds and decided to go for them again."

"Then there's the note."

"The note?" He jerked his head up as London plunged a hand into her purse.

She pulled out a white piece of paper and waved it at him. "I got it last night at the benefit. Someone dropped it onto a waiter's tray and he delivered it to me."

"Would you stop—" he snatched the note from her "—waving things in my face."

He unfolded the notepaper and read aloud. "'Your father was murdered. You could be next.'"

"Looks like they planned to make good on that threat last night." She hunched her shoulders and hugged her waist.

"Why didn't you tell me about this before?"

"The note? I honestly never connected it with the events of last night. I thought the first was an attempted robbery and the second a carjacking. It occurred to me briefly when

I saw Theodore in the hospital this morning and he said something about trying to protect me."

He flicked the paper with his finger. "The wording is weird. 'You *could* be next'? Why didn't he write 'you *are* next'? 'You could be next' implies a conditional situation. You could be next *if* you do this or that."

She snapped her fingers. "That's why I need you."

"The two events are definitely connected, but we don't know if they're related to this warning." He slid one corner of the note beneath the blotter on his desk. "Do you think your father was murdered?"

"I didn't before last night. He had heart disease and he'd already had bypass surgery, but he didn't take care of his health—drank too much, had too much stress and his exercise consisted of walking from his golf cart to the tee."

"Was an autopsy done?"

"For a man as wealthy as my father? Of course. Atherosclerosis—blocked arteries."

"The note could be some kind of scam."

"I thought of that."

"What would the motive be?"

"Money, always money." She hooked a thumb in one pocket of her tight jeans. "So do you accept my proposition? I'll make it worth your while."

He kicked the leg of the single chair opposite his desk. "Have a seat."

She perched on the edge of the wooden chair, clutching the arms. "Does this mean yes?"

"Uh-huh." He yanked open a desk drawer, pulled out a file stuffed with blank contracts and dropped it on the blotter. He raised an eyebrow at her stiff posture. "Relax. I just want to review my terms with you. I'm not gonna require your firstborn or anything."

A blush rushed up her throat, flooding her cheeks and turning her creamy complexion a mottled red.

He needed to tone down the teasing. She couldn't seem to handle it in her agitated state. He also needed to keep this as professional as possible to cool the attraction between them. He'd be no good as a bodyguard if he spent his time lusting after the body he needed to guard.

"Here's my standard contract." He flipped open the file and slid a stapled set of papers toward her. "If you want your attorney to review it…"

"I'm sure it's fine." She plucked it from the desk and flipped through the pages. "Since it's a boilerplate, can we make adjustments as needed? I have several events coming up—there may be some travel."

"Of course. There's a section of the contract that deals with that—page three. Once you review and sign it, I'll ask for a retainer and we can get started."

"How much?" She dipped her hand into her purse and pulled out a checkbook. "I want you to get started right now. I don't need to review the contract. I trust you. You already saved my life once, and you were there for Theodore."

He sat back in his squeaky chair and steepled his fingers. Finding that ski mask had really spooked her, or maybe the note had done the trick.

She didn't even blink an eye when he told her the amount for his retainer. She scribbled out the check and slid it in front of him. "Where do we start?"

"Before we get started, I have a question for you." He picked up the corner of the check and tapped the edge on the blotter. "I'm assuming Breck Global Enterprises has a security force."

"We do."

"Why not enlist their help? You could probably pluck a bodyguard from the staff—someone already vetted and polished up to the BGE standards."

She glanced over her shoulder at the closed door.

"They're not my people. I haven't been at the company that long."

"You don't trust them." This introduced a new twist to the plot. "Who's been running BGE since your father's death? I'm assuming you're still…getting up to speed."

She jumped from the chair and it spun out behind her and hit the wall. "I *am* still getting up to speed, but I'm a fast learner and I'll get there."

"Wow." He raised one eyebrow and settled his boots back on the desk. "You need to chill. If you act this defensive around all the muckety-mucks at BGE, they're going to seriously doubt your abilities even more than they apparently do now."

"Damn." She turned and hit the wall with her palm. "It's just that everywhere I turn, I have people questioning me. It's Dad's fault. He never groomed me to take over the company."

"Did he groom someone else? Another relative?"

She puffed out a breath and swung the chair back in place. "Not really. He acted like he was going to live forever, even after the bypass. My cousin Niles has an interest in the company, and my half brother works there. He's a numbers guy. To answer your previous question before I went ballistic on you, Richard Taylor has been running the show since Dad's death. He and…his son have been my constant companions lately."

He rubbed his knuckles against the stubble of his beard. This looked to be an easy job—expectant relatives or co-workers got their noses out of joint when the old man handed over the reins of his company to his inexperienced daughter, and they decided to use a few threats and scare tactics to get her to decline the responsibility and return to her partying ways.

Gripping the back of the chair, she leaned forward, her silky ponytail falling over her shoulder. She parted her luscious lips and the scent of her expensive perfume washed over him.

This *could* be an easy job, or it could be very, very hard.

"You think you can help me?"

"That's what you're paying me for." He picked up the check and dropped it into his desk drawer. "First things first. I want to have a look at your place, check out the security there. When's a good time for you?"

"Right now, but you saw my building. It's like Fort Knox."

He shoved out of his chair and hunched over his desk. "Are you going to let me do my job, Ms. Breck, or are you going to try to run the show?"

"London. Call me London. After all, we shared a beer and a dance and…other stuff."

It's the other stuff that had him worried. "You didn't answer my question, London."

"I have enough shows to run, Judd. You can have this one."

"You didn't drive over here, did you?"

She snorted. "I didn't want to draw the attention of the paparazzi. So I snuck out and took a taxi."

"Are you okay riding on the back of a bike?"

Her gaze dropped to his boots. "A motorcycle?"

"Yeah."

"I've spent my share of time on the back of motorcycles."

I'll bet you have.

"I'll take you back to your place and have a look around, check out your security and make some notes."

"Sounds good to me."

He locked up the office behind them and followed her downstairs to the street, her high heels clicking on the steps. When they got to his Harley, he unlocked the helmet from the side. "You can wear this. If I get pulled over for not wearing a helmet, I can always have my brother Sean fix the ticket for me."

"Ah, nice to have connections."

"Just kidding." He placed the helmet over her head and buckled the strap beneath her chin. "My brother wouldn't fix a ticket for me or anyone else. Take this, too." He swung his jacket over her shoulders. The wind would blow right through that low-cut sweater.

She shoved her arms through the sleeves and zipped up the jacket.

He straddled the bike and tilted it to the side. "Hop on. I have a backrest, but you might want to hold on while we're going uphill so you don't shift back and forth."

Placing one hand on his shoulder, she climbed onto his Harley. Her knees touched his thighs and she put her hands on either side of his waist while sitting upright. That erect posture wouldn't last long once they started going up and down the hills of the city.

He revved the engine and took off from the curb. When the bike jerked forward, her hands clutched his shirt.

As they idled at a red light, she yelled in his ear. "Do you remember where my place is?"

He nodded once. How could he forget? She lived in one of the most exclusive buildings in the city, in an area where the old robber barons used to have their mansions before the earthquake and fire destroyed most of them.

He climbed a hill with a picture-perfect view of the Transamerica building, and London tightened her grip around his waist as she slid back on the seat. As they rolled down the next hill, her body slammed against his.

"Sorry!" The wind snatched her word and carried it away.

As it should. He didn't need an apology for the pressure of her soft body against his back, her arms wrapped securely around him, the scent of her perfume drugging him. Even her legs tightened against his hips.

He'd have to find another hill to descend.

All too soon he pulled up to the curb in front of her building. He cranked his head over his shoulder. "I'll let you off here and park between those two cars."

He steadied the bike as she clambered off, and then he backed into the space.

She was still fussing with the strap on the helmet when he joined her on the sidewalk.

"Let me. It's a little tricky." He flicked open the catch with his thumb and pulled the helmet from her head.

She tossed her mane of silver hair, which had escaped from her ponytail, back from her flushed face. "Mr. Toad's Wild Ride. That was always my favorite."

"Was it?" A strand of hair clung to the gloss on her mouth and he brushed it aside, the tip of his finger skimming across the smooth skin of her cheek.

Her chest rose and fell as her tongue swept along her bottom lip. Her half-closed lashes fluttered.

If he ever saw an invitation to a kiss, this ranked right up there with the best of them. Did she taste expensive, too? Like Cristal champagne and succulent strawberries?

The cold, hard cash—or at least the cold, hard check she'd written to him that was waiting in his desk drawer—had him pivoting away from her charms. Planting one boot on the step to her building, he smacked the heavy door to the lobby with the palm of his hand. "This is the first line of defense?"

She blinked. "Uh-huh."

He tried the door handle and the solid door didn't budge.

"There's a code." She pointed to the silver keypad to the right of the door, which he'd seen her use last night to gain entry.

"Wait." He held up his hand and started randomly punching buttons on another keypad on the other side of the door.

After several tries, a voice came over the speaker. "Yeah?"

Judd leaned forward. "Forgot my code."

The door clicked and Judd shook his head at London. "Fail."

As they stepped into the marble lobby, she pointed to the security guard at the front desk in front of his monitors. "Backup."

The guard looked up from his magazine and pushed his hat back from his graying hair. "Hello, London."

"Hey, Griff." She wedged her hip against the desk. "Griff, this is Judd Brody. I hired him for some extra security, so you'll be seeing his face around here for a while. Judd, this is Gene Griffin, but we all call him Griff."

The older man didn't even rise from his chair, and Judd leaned over to shake his hand. "Retired cop?"

Griff grinned. "That obvious?"

Obvious he'd found himself a cushy job while collecting his pension. "I have a couple of brothers who are cops—it's just the look."

He walked behind Griff and hovered over his shoulder. "Why is that monitor dark?"

"Couldn't tell you. I'm not the tech guy. It's been reported and someone's going to come out to work on it."

"Which area does it cover?"

"The garage, I think." He slapped his magazine down on the desk and tapped a few keys on the keyboard, which did nothing at all. "Yeah, that's the garage."

"What are your shifts here?"

Griff shot a look beneath shaggy eyebrows at London, who lifted one shoulder. "Eight to four, four to midnight, and midnight to eight. It's twenty-four-hour coverage."

"Do you ever leave the desk?"

The guard picked up his celebrity magazine and shook it out. "When nature calls, buddy."

"Lunch? Patrols around the building?"

"Yep."

"Any coverage when that happens?"

"Nope."

Judd rapped on the desk with his knuckles. "Thanks for the info, Griff."

He hadn't meant to piss off the old guy, but some people took his tone the wrong way. Hell, London had hired him to protect her, not make nice with lazy security guards. The guys on the night shifts had to be better.

As he followed London across the lobby to the elevators, he glanced up at the cameras in the corners—visible and easy to dismantle or block.

London stabbed at the elevator call button and hissed, "Why were you interrogating Griff like that? He's a good guy."

"He's a retired cop who found himself an easy gig where he can sit on his ass and read celebrity rags."

"Shh." She put a finger to her lips, her sculpted eyebrows colliding over her nose.

The elevator doors whispered open and he stepped into the mirrored car after London. "Just calling it like it is. I'm here to assess the risks to your security and I just found two of them. You don't let random strangers into the building just because they buzz your place, do you?"

"No, sir." She trailed a finger across her left breast. "Cross my heart."

He dragged his gaze away from her cleavage and backed up against one mirrored wall. "Good, because that's just stupid. What's the point of having a coded key entry?"

"No point at all."

"Are you making fun of me? Because this is serious. This is your security."

Her smile twitched at one corner. "It's just that you got all stern on me and poor Griff."

God, he must've come across like his brothers. He folded his arms across his chest. "Just doing my job, ma'am."

"And I appreciate that."

The elevator dinged to a stop and the doors slid open onto a quiet hallway. The shiny marble from the lobby had been replaced by carpet so thick his boot would probably leave a crater in the pile.

"How many places up here?" He glanced down the hallway. Technically she had the penthouse, since her place occupied the top floor of the building, but it looked as if she shared the space with at least one other unit.

"Two." She had her keys in her hand.

"Who's your neighbor?"

"I don't have one."

"Is the other place for sale?"

"No." She spun around at her door. "I own the other place. I bought it when the previous owner gave it up."

He held up his hands at her defensive tone. "Hey, I'd do the same."

She shoved her key into the dead bolt and froze. "Judd."

"What?"

"I always lock my dead bolt, and it's not locked."

Adrenaline shot through his system and he reached for the weapon in his gun bag. "Step back, London. Let me go through first."

She unlocked the door handle and he twisted it. He raised his gun, easing the door open.

He took in the scene before him. Either London Breck was one messy heiress or her place had been tossed.

She gasped behind him and let loose with a string of profanities.

Her place had been tossed.

Chapter Five

London pushed past Judd's solid frame, but he grabbed her around the waist before she hit the foyer, nearly lifting her off her feet.

"Hold on. We have no idea if the perpetrator is still here or not."

"Perpetrator?" Her blood simmered and she felt like putting her fist through the wall. "I've got a few other choice names for him."

"Yeah, you just screamed them in my ear." He tugged on his earlobe and tilted his head back. "How big is this place?"

"Big."

Judd kept his gun in front of him, and she almost wished the SOB was still here so he could get a load of that.

"Okay, stay with me and we'll do a sweep of the place, unless you want to leave now and call the cops."

"I'm hoping we catch him in the act. I'm not waiting for the cops."

"All right, Calamity Jane, just stay behind me in case he is."

She stayed close to Judd as she directed him through the rooms of the condo, each one ransacked and upended. They even looked in the closets and under the beds, but the slimeball had done his dirty work and escaped.

He replaced his gun in what she assumed was an out-of-character fanny pack and hooked a thumb in one belt loop. "Now that we know he's not here, do you want to see what's missing? I'll get on the phone and call the cops."

Crooking her finger at him, she marched across the great room and through the double doors to the library. She placed both hands against a bookshelf and shoved. It turned into the wall, exposing a cavity with a squat metal safe in the center.

Judd whistled. "That's some James Bond stuff right there."

She aimed the pointed toe of her boot at the safe. "All my important papers and real jewelry are in there, except for the important papers and real jewelry in some safe-deposit boxes."

"Check it just to make sure."

She crouched in front of the safe and he turned away while she spun the dial on the combination lock. He *did* take his job seriously.

The safe opened with a heavy click and she pulled open the door. "You can peek now."

He squatted on the floor beside her, his hands braced on his muscled thighs, his shoulder brushing hers. They were almost as close as they'd been on that motorcycle. Every time he'd gone downhill, which had seemed to happen a lot, the decline had thrown her against his back. She'd fought mightily against resting her head against his shoulder and exploring beneath his shirt with her hands.

That ride, with him between her legs and the monster machine buzzing beneath her, had been about the most sensuous journey she'd ever experienced.

Only to come to a screeching halt when they reached her ransacked apartment.

He cocked his head, and his long black hair tickled her cheek. "Well?"

She plunged her hands into the recesses of the safe and grabbed stacks of paper bonds, bringing them into the light. She tossed them back inside and her fingers curled around a velvet box, which she pulled out and dropped to the floor. She flicked the latch and the jewels inside glittered in the muted light.

"Did you get those from the queen of England or something?" He reached into the box and hooked a finger around a necklace of rubies with pink diamonds clustered around each one.

"My father bought that for my mother. I have no idea where he got it." She wrinkled her nose. "It's not my style."

He dropped it. "Not mine, either. I guess your taste runs more toward three-hundred-carat yellow diamonds."

She sucked in a breath. So he *did* know all about her. Well, not everything. "Sheikh al Sayid gave that diamond to me. Of course he was going to deny it when his wife found out—*one* of his wives, I may add."

"The question is, what did you do to earn it?"

"You have a dirty mind." She punched him in the shoulder and then shook her fist. Was the man hard all over?

He wasn't the only one with a dirty mind.

"Any other treasures in there?"

There were, but a few she'd keep to herself.

"There's nothing missing from this safe." She slammed the door shut and fell to her backside. "Whatever else he might've taken—cameras, computers, gadgets—he's welcome to them."

"Computers? If he has your computers, you could be in for a lot of trouble."

"All company information and financials are stored on computers at the office. I don't do any of that at home, not even on a laptop. I have a backup service, so I'm not going to lose any music or pictures." She covered her mouth with her hand. There were pictures she didn't want anyone to see—not even some junkie thief.

"What is it?"

Judd had moved closer, his knees bumping hers.

She looked into his eyes, the darkness of the room casting them the color of a deep ocean-blue. She probably should tell him everything, come clean about everything. No. Maddie had nothing to do with any of this, and she didn't need Judd Brody thinking of her as any more flighty than he already did, or worse, as someone heartless and selfish.

"Getting all those files restored would be a major pain."

Pushing to his feet, he extended his hand. "Then let's go see what's missing, and I'll call the cops." He circled his finger around the safe room. "I wouldn't mention this, though—to anyone."

"Nobody knows about it except me and you. My father had it put in when I bought this place."

She grasped his hand and he pulled her up. The small room had them inches apart and she breathed in the scent of him—soapy with a hint of mint from his warm breath—and something else. Something she couldn't identify, but that made her think of tousled sheets and bare skin and bruised lips.

Must be all the heightened tension of the break-in, but he could take her right here and she wouldn't complain one bit. She'd make it a point to be the best he ever had—and from his looks and manner, he'd had more than his share.

He kicked the door of the safe closed with a bang and she jumped. "The rest of your stuff?"

His harsh tone brought her back to reality. He'd made it pretty clear he didn't want to take her here or anywhere. Not that he didn't enjoy the sparks between them—she could read a man as well as the next girl—but he had no intention of lighting that fuse.

She bent forward and it was his turn to jump back. She flattened out her smile as she twirled the dial of the safe. "Just locking up."

Squeezing past her, he backed out of the room, his thigh brushing against her bum.

"Claustrophobic in there." He let out a long breath and raked his fingers through his long hair.

He helped her swing the bookcase back into place, and she turned to survey the rest of the library. The monitor for the desktop computer was askew, and she looked beneath the desk for the CPU.

"One computer gone."

"I suppose he had to take something to make it look good."

"What are you saying?" She placed her hand on his forearm, her nails digging into the ink of his tattoos.

"London, this is obviously linked to the previous threats. Someone is trying to spook you or warn you. This is not some garden-variety break-in. I thought you'd figured that out the minute we walked into the condo."

"I guess I did." She twisted a strand of hair around one finger. She hadn't really thought about who was responsible and why. That white-hot anger thumping through her veins had blotted out everything else, but it made sense.

"So you don't think whoever broke in is really interested in what's on my computer?"

"I can't know for sure, but this seems like another scare tactic—he can get to you."

"Where's the demand? If he wants me to do or not do something, how am I supposed to know what that is?"

"Maybe he figures you'll get so stressed out, you'll drop the whole idea of running BGE."

It must be someone who knew her well, then, because that was exactly what she would've done in the past. When the going got tough, London Breck threw up her hands and took a vacation. The *old* London Breck.

"I don't know, Judd." She left the library and checked the kitchen table, where she usually kept her laptop. "My laptop's gone, too."

A little fizz of fear made its way up her spine. Whoever had that laptop could make some interesting deductions from the pictures she kept on there.

She poked around and discovered other items missing— small electronics, some costume jewelry, three designer handbags—little stuff. Personal effects that would indicate a quickie burglary by someone who needed cash.

Slumping on the couch, she tilted her head back against the cushion and closed her eyes. "Are the cops on their way?"

"Eventually. I'm going to have a talk with Griff before they get here."

"Great. He'll probably never speak to me again."

"He should lose his job. It happened on his so-called watch."

"Please." She opened one eye. "Do not get him fired."

"Afraid of being labeled Ms. Scrooge? I'm sure the other tenants in this building are going to want to know about this." He sat on the arm of the couch. "I wouldn't worry too much about old Griff. He's collecting a nice pension. He's not going to starve in the streets."

"I'm not going to be responsible for anyone losing a job."

"Oh, boy." He flicked her earlobe. "How are you going to run a multibillion-dollar global company?"

"I haven't figured that out yet. Any ideas?"

"Me? I don't even have a filing system down for my business."

She trudged after Judd through the lobby, keeping her focus on his nice backside to avoid thinking about the conversation ahead and everything else going wrong in her life right now. If he didn't want her jumping his bones, why did he wear jeans like that? Why did his blue eyes smolder when he looked at her? Why did his long hair brush his collar, asking to be smoothed away?

"Griff, we have a problem."

Griff peeked over the top of his magazine. "You again."

"Someone broke into Ms. Breck's condo, ransacked the place and stole some items."

Griff's eyes bugged out from their sockets and his magazine dropped to the floor. "Th-that's not possible."

"It's not only possible—" Judd hunched over the table, the muscles in his arms flexing, his tattoos dancing "—it's a fact. What time did you vacate your station after Ms. Breck left this morning?"

"Vacate?" His previously bulging eyes narrowed. "You make it sound like I did something on purpose."

Judd straightened up to his full height and crossed his arms over his formidable chest. "Why would you say something like that? *Did* you do something on purpose?"

"I don't know what the hell you're talking about." He shook his finger at Judd. "Don't think I don't know who you are. Brody."

He practically spit out the name, and Judd's posture grew more rigid. Danger shimmered from him in waves.

London's quick glance at Griff confirmed that he felt it, too. His face reddened and the muscles seemed to go slack, but he carried on.

"Your brother and that true-crime writer might've exonerated Joey Brody, but I don't believe it. If he didn't do all those people as the Phone Book Killer, why'd he off himself, huh? Why'd he take a dive off the Golden Gate?"

A muscle in Judd's jaw twitched, and London raised a shaky hand—as if she could stop a panther once he went into attack mode.

A pounding on the front door made them all stop and

turn around. Two uniformed officers cupped their hands on the glass and peered into the lobby.

Griff couldn't open the door fast enough. He fumbled for the button beneath his desk and the doors clicked.

The cops strolled in and the older one asked, "Are you London Breck? Your place was robbed?"

"That's right." She approached them, extending her hand. "We were just—ah—talking to the security guard to find out if he noticed anything."

The officer shook her hand. "I'm Officer Jessup and this is Officer Spann."

Judd broke away from the desk. "I'm Judd Brody. I'm working security for Ms. Breck."

Jessup coughed. "That's a coincidence. Have you had previous break-ins, Ms. Breck? Is that the reason for hiring a P.I.?"

She didn't even bother to ask how he knew Judd was a private investigator and not just a security guard. It seemed as if the entire law enforcement community knew about the Brody brothers.

"Not a break-in, but I've been having some issues ever since my father passed away."

"Of course. Sorry for your loss, ma'am. Your father was a big supporter of the SFPD. We'll miss him."

"Thank you."

Officer Spann had parked himself in front of the security desk and a visibly shaken Griff. "Did you notice anything?"

"No. I did my rounds, as usual. Took a few breaks." He shot a glance at Judd. "Which is allowed."

The cop tapped the top of one of the monitors. "You have security cameras and footage, right?"

"Yeah, when they work." He jerked his thumb at the dark screen. "This one's been on the fritz."

"Can we have a look at those right now?"

While Officer Spann hung over Griff's shoulder at the

security desk, Officer Jessup pulled a notepad from his pocket. "What did he take, Ms. Breck?"

"A couple of computers, some costume jewelry, a camcorder." She held up her hand, ticking the items off on each finger. "I can get you a list, the same one I'm sending to my insurance company."

He turned to Judd. "Any sign of forced entry?"

"No. He picked the lock or had a key." His gaze wandered toward Griff, who was tapping the keyboard and jabbing his finger at the monitors.

Judd really had it in for Griff, especially now after that jab at his father. Judd had told her he'd put the past behind him, that it didn't matter, but his reaction told another story.

She cleared her throat. "I doubt he had a key, or he would've locked the dead bolt behind him, and he didn't do that."

"Or maybe he didn't lock the dead bolt because he didn't want you know he had a key."

"We'll come up and have a look." Jessup tilted his head back to take in the high ceiling of the lobby. "If you're on the top floor of this building, he didn't climb through the window."

"Jessup, you gotta see this." Spann looked up from the security desk, over Griff's red face.

London's pulse jumped. "Is he on the video?"

"Not only is he not on it, nobody's on it. The lobby camera hasn't been recording anything all morning."

London stamped her foot. "That figures. What is the point of having cameras when they're always breaking down?"

"Exactly." Judd's eyes glittered like chips of agate.

Griff's Adam's apple bobbed in his flushed throat.

Tugging on Judd's sleeve, London said, "Let's show the cops my place. Maybe they can get some fingerprints."

The officers checked the door and surveyed the mess,

but they couldn't get fingerprints or tell her anything more about the break-in. She promised them the complete list of stolen items, but had no hope of getting any of them back.

When the cops left, London collapsed on the couch. "They'll never see my stuff in a pawnshop, will they? That's not why the thief or thieves stole it."

"You're catching on." Judd paced in front of her. "They wanted it to look like a burglary, but we both know they just wanted to scare you."

She kicked her feet up onto the coffee table. "They're going to have to do more than that to get me to give up control of BGE."

"That's what worries me, London. If I don't find these guys now, what else do they have planned for you?"

"They'll slip up—maybe next time."

"I don't want there to be a next time. I need to find them now." He punched his fist into his palm. "And I know a good place to start."

He turned toward the door and she jumped up. "You're not going to harass Griff again, are you?"

His eyebrows spiked. "Harass? He knows something, London. Do you think it's just a coincidence that the cameras failed this morning at precisely the time someone gained entry to the building to break into your place?"

"Wait. You're telling me he's working with these guys?"

"Why is that so hard to believe? The guy has a good pension and benefits from the city and he's still working as a security guard? He obviously needs money."

He swung open the door and she rushed to follow him. "I'm coming with you so someone doesn't wind up in the emergency room."

When Judd burst onto the lobby floor, Griff's mouth gaped open.

"What do you want? I told everything to the cops and I'm not saying any more, especially to you."

Judd lunged over the security desk and grabbed the front of the man's shirt. He pulled him from his chair. "You are going to talk to me—right now."

Griff choked and coughed. "Let me go."

Judd shook him like a rag doll and then dropped him in his chair. "Why did you turn that camera off? Who did you let in here? Who paid you?"

Griff scooted his chair back. "You're crazy, violent, just like your old man."

Wrong thing to say. Griff was either brave or stupid. London held her breath.

That stillness fell over Judd again, and then he whipped around the desk with a quickness and agility that didn't match his size.

He yanked Griff out of his chair again and slammed him against the wall.

Mrs. Schrader and a friend came through the lobby doors and tripped to a stop.

"Everything okay, London?"

"Uh, my place was broken into this morning. The cops are just trying to get some answers from Griff."

If Mrs. Schrader and her friend wondered at this so-called cop's methods, they didn't seem to want to inquire further. They scurried toward the elevator without a backward glance.

Judd dug his hand into the front pocket of Griff's pants and pulled out a thick envelope. He tossed it onto the desk—a few bills peeked from it.

"Where'd you get that, huh?"

Griff slumped against the wall. "I didn't know they were going to break into your place, London. I swear."

"What? Someone paid you to let them in the building and then mess with the lobby camera?"

"Yeah." Griff sank to his chair. "It wasn't the first time, and nothing like a robbery ever happened before."

"You've done this before?" Judd stepped to the other side of the desk, flexing his fingers.

"Yeah."

"Why?" London felt like sitting down herself.

He prodded the envelope with his finger. "Money. It's only the paps. That's who I thought it was this time. That's what they told me."

"The paps?" Judd's eyebrows collided over his nose. "The paparazzi?"

The color rushed into Griff's face again. "They pay good money to get into places like this. Sorry, London. I didn't think there was any harm. They usually just want a few pictures, maybe to dig around your trash. I've worked with Ray Lopez before, and he's a good guy."

"My trash?" She felt as if she needed a shower.

"It's not just you, London. There are a few others in this building they want. You know who."

Judd landed his fist on the desk. "This time they wanted to break into her place. What if they wanted to kill someone? Would you be okay with that, too?"

"Kill someone?" He shook his head back and forth. "They just want information, a scoop. You know, like Ray Lopez."

"The men who broke into London's place weren't paparazzi, you idiot."

Griff's eyes popped open. "Of course they were. They told me they were."

"How long were you a cop?" Judd ran a hand through his hair.

"I've done this kind of thing before and never had a problem."

Judd propped up the wall with his shoulder as if to box Griff in. "What did they look like, these two paparazzi?"

"I—I don't know."

"What?"

Griff folded his arms over his paunch. "They were wearing disguises. You know, caps, sunglasses, facial hair."

Judd's mouth fell open. "And you didn't think that was weird?"

"Naw. They do that all the time." Griff smacked his magazine. "They have to go to extremes to get the good pics."

"Can you at least write down their height, build, accent… disguises?"

Griff pulled a piece of paper in front of him and started writing.

When he handed the descriptions over, Judd shoved the paper in his pocket and asked, "Did they at least give you back the key?"

"I didn't give them any key." Griff spread his hands. "I swear, London. They just asked for the number of your place and floor."

She turned to Judd. "Then they picked the locks?"

"Probably." Judd hunched over the desk. "Did you see them leave?"

"That was part of the deal. I made myself scarce." Griff chewed on the side of his thumb. "Do you have to report this to management, London?"

"Griff, it's completely out of my control. The management company has to know there was a burglary in the building and why."

He heaved a heavy sigh and leaned back in his chair. "Guess I'll be looking for another gig."

Judd took her arm. "Let's go back up. I have one more thing I want to check."

This time when she put the key in the dead bolt, it clicked. "At least they didn't sneak back in while we were downstairs." She surveyed the mess. "I'll start cleaning up. What else did you need?"

Prowling around the room, checking lamp shades and pictures, Judd answered, "I'm doing a cursory check for bugs—audio and visual. I have equipment that can do a more thorough job, and I'll be bringing that over."

"Ugh." London shivered. "That's a creepy thought."

"I think they broke in today just to give you another scare, make you think twice about stepping into your father's shoes. But if you don't give up, spying on you could be an effective weapon in their arsenal against you. I've dealt with corporate spying before—it's not unusual."

London dipped her head. If the burglars got a load of the pictures on her laptop, they just might have another weapon in their arsenal against her.

She replaced cushions and reshelved books while Judd continued his search for bugs—much scarier ones than spiders.

When he finished, he stood in the middle of the great room. "I didn't find anything, but I'm going to come back tomorrow with my equipment for a more thorough check."

Sounded as though he planned to leave—not that she believed she could keep him here forever. "I should be around in the afternoon."

"Get the locks changed tomorrow as a precaution and leave a new key for me with security."

"Right. Come whenever you like." She waved her arms around the room. "I'll keep putting things together tonight."

"Let me know if you discover anything else missing— or anything out of order."

"I will. Thanks for everything, Judd. Without your perseverance, we never would've gotten the truth out of Griff."

"Glad you see it that way." He scooped up his jacket and helmet. "I'll be in touch tomorrow."

She closed the door behind him and locked it. If he hadn't been with her today, she would've freaked out walking in on this mess alone. In hiring Judd Brody to have her back, she'd made the first in what she planned to be a long line of good decisions.

London spent the rest of the afternoon cleaning up without discovering any other missing items—or bugs.

When her stomach growled for about the hundredth time, she realized she'd completely skipped lunch. She should've invited Judd out for lunch, but she hadn't wanted to be too forward or cross the line with him.

He seemed hung up on their working relationship and she should be hung up on it, too. Professional people knew the line between business and pleasure and adhered to it. If she wanted to step up as the CEO of BGE, she'd better start acting like a professional.

If Judd Brody could keep his lust zipped up while they worked together, so could she.

Her cell phone buzzed and she swept it off the counter, checking the display. "Hi, April."

"Hi, just checking to see if you're still going to that new club with us tonight."

London opened the sliding doors to the balcony and stepped outside. "I'm going to pass."

April wailed, "You're turning into a drudge, London. Gemma's cousin is in from Monte Carlo, and he's really interested in meeting you."

"Is this the gambler? I bet he's really interested in meeting me."

"Oh, stop. He has money of his own. Not every man is after your big bucks. Do not tell me you're seriously considering Roger Taylor's proposal. Just because he's über-rich, that doesn't make him a perfect match for you."

A flash of blue eyes and the revving engine of a Harley made it clear that Roger could never be her perfect match. "Don't worry. I'm not that much of a drudge. Someone broke into my place today and I've spent all afternoon cleaning up—not the best prelude to a night out."

April gasped. "What did he take?"

"Nothing of importance." Except that laptop. "But I'm not in any mood to go clubbing."

"I hear ya. I'll tell you all about the new place and the new man."

"Have fun, April." London cradled the phone in her hands and gazed at the lights blinking on in the city. She still needed to eat, but she didn't feel like venturing out and she didn't want to cook. She punched in the number for the local pizza place and ordered a large vegetarian pizza.

By the time the pizza had arrived, she'd taken a quick shower and changed into yoga pants and a light hoodie. She spoke into the intercom. "I'll be right down."

She grabbed some bills from her purse, locked the door behind her and headed down to the lobby in the elevator.

Jerome, the night security guard, had his eye on the delivery guy as if half expecting him to pull a gun out of the pizza box.

London exchanged the cash for the pizza and thanked the delivery boy.

When he left, she placed the pizza on top of the security desk. "I suppose you heard what happened this morning."

Jerome shook his head. "I always thought Griff was trouble—him and those celebrity rags. Shoulda figured he'd be one of those guys selling stories and stuff."

"Do you know if he's been fired?"

"Not sure. I guess we'll find out come eight o'clock tomorrow morning." Jerome straightened his shoulders. "I hope you know I'd never do anything like that, Ms. Breck."

"I know that. It's just crazy Griff didn't think about the consequences."

He pointed to the pizza box. "No fancy shindig tonight, huh?"

"I don't know, Jerome." She wrapped her fingers around the edges of the pizza box. "I think my fancy shindig days are over."

She carried the pizza up to her place and settled it on the kitchen counter. She had a few files to go over before tomorrow's shareholder meeting and would try not to get tomato sauce on them.

A few hours later, she put the leftover pizza into the fridge and scrunched her paper plate in the trash.

Her phone buzzed again, once. If April thought she could talk her into going out, she had it all wrong, even if the man from Monte Carlo had turned out to be a winner.

She washed her hands and retrieved her phone to check the text message. Take out the trash.

Her brow furrowed. Who had sent that? She squinted at the display—blocked. Must be a wrong number.

The text indicator buzzed again and she smirked. Some husband was going to be in big trouble tonight for not taking out the trash.

Yawning, she slipped the phone into the front pouch of her hoodie. It buzzed again, tickling her tummy.

She pulled it out and typed in a reply—wrong number.

As she wiped the crumbs from the counter, another text came through. She tossed the dish towel into the sink and dragged out the phone again.

She froze. Take out the trash, LONDON.

Was this some kind of joke? Had April had one of her fellow club hoppers text her? But what did it mean?

The phone continued to buzz in her hand as the text came through over and over. Take out the trash? She glanced at the empty pizza box. She had to take out the trash anyway.

She tucked the pizza box beneath one arm and grabbed her key. With the text message indicator still buzzing, she locked her door behind her and trudged to the end of the hallway to the little room that contained the trash chute.

She licked her lips and shoved open the door. The silver lid of the trash chute gleamed in the dim closet. She lifted the lid with two fingers and the smell of garbage wafted into the small space. Wrinkling her nose, she dropped the pizza box down the black hole and let the lid fall back into place.

The clang resounded in the closet.

She pulled out her phone and spoke to it. "There, are you happy?"

It must be April playing some kind of joke. Maybe she'd meant take out the trash and make room for a new man? It had to be April.

When London got back to her condo, she tapped April's name in her contact list with a less-than-steady finger.

April answered with a breathless voice. "Change your mind?"

"No. Who's sending me texts about the trash?" She held her breath, hoping for April's laughing admission of guilt.

"What?"

"Are you having someone text me messages about taking out the trash?"

"London, what are you talking about? Look, I'm in a taxi on my way to the Bay Club for cocktails. Then it's off to the new place. If you've changed your mind, meet us there."

"You didn't put someone up to texting me?" Her voice rose to an unnatural high note.

"About trash? No. You're losing it."

She just might be. While she'd been on the phone to April, the text had come through five more times.

What trash? Was her stolen stuff in the trash? Had the burglars had second thoughts? Maybe they'd seen the police here. How the hell had they gotten her number?

All the trash chutes on this side of the building led to a larger bin in a room off the lobby. Was that the trash she should check? She didn't want to do it alone.

Jerome was downstairs. He could come with her.

Once again, she pocketed her still-buzzing phone and

left her condo. A couple got into the elevator with her on the third floor and she nodded at them.

The woman jabbed the button for the lobby. "Did someone break into your place today?"

"Yeah. Turns out Griff was giving the paparazzi access to our building."

The woman's nostrils flared and she sniffed. "That's very unfortunate. I hope he's gone."

"I think he is." Thanks to Judd.

The elevator opened onto the lobby, and the couple continued out the front door, where a town car waited for them.

Jerome looked up from the monitor. "More pizza, London?"

"No, I keep getting a weird text from some unknown person telling me to check the trash. I looked into the chute upstairs, but there's nothing there."

He raised his eyebrows. "Just because you get a text from someone doesn't mean you have to do what it says."

"I know." She placed a shaky hand over the buzzing phone in her pocket. "I just have a feeling—maybe my missing stuff is in the trash bin down here. Can you check it out with me?"

His gaze darted between the empty lobby and the working monitors on the security desk. "I don't want to leave my post, especially since Griff basically broke the camera down here and there's no coverage on the lobby, and there's still no coverage on the garage."

She turned toward the door that led to the trash room and crossed her arms. "I'm still a little on edge after the break-in."

"Tell you what—" Jerome reached under the security desk and held up two slanted blocks of wood "—prop the doors open with these. I can sort of see into the hallway."

"That'll work." She took the doorstops from him and

marched toward the first door. She shoved open the door and kicked one piece of wood beneath it to hold it open.

The chill from the cement floor in the hallway caused a rash of goose bumps to spread across her arms. She eyed the metal door at the end of the hallway. "The trash room is that door at the end, right?"

"Yeah. Prop that one open, too, when you get there."

"Sure thing." Her voice rang out brighter than she felt. Maybe she should just turn off her phone, forget the whole thing tonight and have Judd trace the call tomorrow.

The phone buzzed again with the same message, as if taunting her. If she planned to hold on to her job and execute her responsibilities at BGE, she'd have to show these goons they didn't scare her.

"Okay, I'm heading down the hallway. Maybe management should put a camera over here, too."

Jerome called back from the lobby, sounding very far away. "I'll suggest it. There's nothing out there or in the alley where the garbage trucks pull up."

London threw back her shoulders and proceeded down the corridor, her flip-flops smacking the cement. She grabbed the handle and pressed down, nudging the door with her hip. It opened with a creak.

"This door needs oil." She cocked her head. "Jerome?"

"I hear ya. Maybe I'll suggest that, too. You see anything in there?"

"Just a couple of big trash bins." She pinched her nose.

A soft, rhythmic tapping sound had her stumbling backward. "Are there rats out here?"

"I hope not, or that's another suggestion."

Crouching down, she shoved the doorstop in place and rose slowly, brushing her fingers against her yoga pants.

A bag of trash hurtled down the chute and London pressed a hand against her heart. "Scared me."

"What?"

"Nothing, just some trash coming down."

"It *is* the trash room."

She grabbed the edge of the bin and found a foothold on the edge, peering inside. Yep, trash. No computers, no camcorders, no jewelry.

Someone had decided to yank her chain with those texts—maybe the burglars, maybe not.

The tapping noise started again and she jumped off the bin. Her gaze wandered to the other door in the room. "Jerome?"

"You done in there?"

"Yeah...no." She took a step toward the metal door. The tapping had turned into a soft scraping sound coming from the other side of that door.

"What's this door in here?"

"Leads to the alley, same as the sliding door. We roll up the sliding door on garbage day so the trash collectors can pick up the bin and empty it.

She hadn't noticed the warehouse-style corrugated metal door behind the bin.

"I-is it locked?"

"Just from the inside, but what do you want to go outside for?"

"There's a noise out there."

"Probably cats."

"Probably." She edged toward the door and placed her hand on the cold handle. She swallowed and pushed it open.

The door hit something hanging from above. Looking up, she peered around the edge of the door and then wished she hadn't.

A man's lifeless body hung from the awning above the door—a celebrity magazine sticking out of his pocket.

Chapter Six

Judd rubbed circles on London's back as she rocked back and forth. Every once in a while, she'd stop rocking and a tremble would roll through her body. When that happened, her teeth would chatter and she'd hunch her shoulders, giving him the urge to take her lithe form in his arms.

He resisted the urge.

The SFPD homicide detective, one of his brother's colleagues, tapped the plastic bag containing London's phone. "We can trace the texts, but most likely it'll come back to a throwaway phone. People who commit murder do not leave messages from traceable phones."

Judd's hand paused on London's back. "You're probably right, but it's worth a try. You might get lucky."

Unlike Griff. The SOB had gotten involved with the wrong people. He thought he'd hit the jackpot and picked up some extra cash. Now the crime-scene techs were downstairs and the coroner was probably on his way.

Detective Curtis planted his hands on his knees and pushed to his feet. "Thanks for the info, Judd. Why someone, especially a former cop, would allow a couple of guys wearing obvious disguises into an exclusive building like this one is beyond me."

Judd got to his feet and shook Curtis's hand. "I guess your pensions aren't big enough. Griff did it for the money."

"You said he had an envelope stuffed with bills?"

"Yeah, payment from the burglars."

"Well, whoever killed him took that off him, too."

London raised a pair of wide eyes, peering at them through a veil of hair. "Griff didn't have a family, did he? He never mentioned a wife and kids to me."

"I'm not sure, Ms. Breck. We've contacted his employer for next of kin, although the other security guard said Griff had been divorced for a while."

Judd saw Curtis to London's front door since she'd retreated behind her hair and the blanket he'd draped around her shoulders.

"You take care, Ms. Breck. I called Captain Williams at home to let him know what happened, and he was glad I did. We'll notify you if anything breaks. In the meantime, I'm leaving you in good hands."

Judd thanked Curtis and returned to London's side. "How about a glass of wine? Some tea? Water?"

Her head jerked up. "I didn't hear your conversation with Detective Curtis earlier. Was Griff dead before they strung him up or d-did they hang him?"

"You didn't hear that conversation for a reason. Do you really need to know that?" She needed wine, and he wandered into her vast kitchen to look for a bottle.

"Yes." She knotted her fingers and he could see how unsettled she was. "I need to know everything."

He banged open a few cupboards. "Wine?"

"In the wine cellar."

Oh, yeah, he vaguely remembered a step-down room, dark and oaky, filled with racks upon racks of bottles.

She must've noticed the confusion crossing his face, because she flicked her fingers toward the kitchen. "There's a top-rated *Wine Spectator* pinot grigio open in the fridge."

Of course, pinot grigio in the fridge. Who didn't have a

Wine Spectator top-rated pinot grigio in the fridge? Whatever the hell that meant.

He pulled open the door, grabbed the bottle of wine off the top shelf and snagged himself a top-rated Judd Brody bottle of beer in the process. She could open a bar with the stock she had on hand, and a coffee shop with all the coffee gadgets littering the kitchen, and probably a flower shop to top it off.

He lifted a glass from the cupboard, poured in the wine and twisted off the beer bottle's cap. He needed a drink after his epic fail. He'd figured the intruders had broken in as another scare tactic, but they'd just added murder to their repertoire—and they'd wanted to make sure London found the body.

Why?

Were they really threatening her life if she didn't give up control of BGE? He'd have to take a look at the players in that corporation, although it could be someone outside the corporation—a competitor or disgruntled former employee.

He sat down next to London and placed her glass on the coffee table in front of her. She deserved to know what she was facing.

"They killed Griff before they hanged him. They choked him, probably with a garrote."

She took a gulp of wine and pressed the back of her hand to her lips. "Why?"

"So he wouldn't identify them, because he talked to the cops, or maybe just to get rid of him and tie up loose ends."

"Do you think Griff was telling the truth about the disguises? Maybe they didn't have hats and beards. Maybe they'd just warned Griff to keep quiet and he had no intention of telling us anything about them."

"If so, he misplaced his loyalties." He rolled the damp beer bottle between his palms. "Who's Captain Williams? The name sounds familiar."

"He's a captain in homicide. Your brother probably knows him. He and my father go way back, and he's been trying to get the chief's position for years."

"Williams, yeah." He took a sip of beer. "You need to replace your phone, get a new phone number."

"I'll do that tomorrow."

"Today." He tapped his watch. "It's after midnight."

She ran her fingertip around the rim of her glass. "I'm used to the general trouble fame causes—paparazzi, media, gossip. But this…it's serious."

"Damn straight it is. It was serious when they beat Theodore to a pulp, and now it's deadly serious."

"I don't understand what they want. Why don't they, whoever they are, give me some demands?"

"Maybe they don't have any demands."

"You mean they just want to kill me?" She threw back another gulp of wine.

"I don't think so. It's not as though they didn't have their chances to do that—in the hotel alley, here in your place or down in that trash room—an idiotic move on your part, by the way. Why would you go down there on your own after what's been happening?"

He saw the color rise in her face when he called her actions idiotic. "I planned to take Jerome with me, and he was right in the next room."

"Not close enough." He chugged the rest of his beer and stretched. "I'm staying here tonight."

Her wine sloshed over the rim of the glass. "I beg your pardon?"

"I'm going to camp out—" he bounced his fist on the cushion next to him "—right here."

"Do I have to pay extra for that service?"

"You'll see it on my bill."

"If I'm going to be charged for the twenty-four-hour

coverage, you might as well stay in style. I have several guest rooms, beds already made up."

"I think I need to stay right here. Unless, of course, this is a top-rated *Couch Spectator* couch."

Even though the strain of the evening still clouded her eyes, the corner of her mouth lifted in a smile. "You don't want to know how much that couch cost, but you're welcome to it—as long as you remove your motorcycle boots."

"I'll remove more than my motorcycle boots."

He ignored the look from her narrowed eyes and pushed up from the couch with his empty beer bottle in one hand. "If you're going to be ready for your meeting tomorrow morning, you'd better get a good night's sleep. And since I'm going with you to the office, I'm going to hit the sack, too."

She reached for her glass, almost knocking it over, but swooped in before it hit the table. "Y-you're coming with me?"

"Yep."

"In what capacity?"

"Bodyguard."

"Should I introduce you as my bodyguard?"

"Sweetheart, you can introduce me as whatever you want or don't introduce me at all, but you should keep mum about the activities of the past few days."

"I'm probably not going to be able to hide the fact that a security guard was murdered in my building and I found him."

"So? Your involvement ends there. Don't you ever keep secrets?"

"Sure." She jumped from the couch and turned toward the kitchen. "I'll get you a blanket and pillow for the couch."

She rinsed her glass in the sink and then disappeared upstairs.

True to his promise, Judd sat down and pulled off his boots. He stuffed his socks inside and placed them beside the couch. Then he chucked a few throw pillows onto the floor to make some room. The couch had to be six feet long, but that still wouldn't accommodate him from head to toe.

No doubt he'd find more comfort in one of London's guest rooms, but he could keep better watch down here by the front door, and he didn't want to be in some soft, comfortable bed with London in her soft, comfortable bed somewhere down the hall. He didn't need the distraction.

"I brought a sheet to tuck in around the couch and a blanket and pillow. Do you think you'll need another blanket?"

"You keep the temperature warm in here. I'm good."

She shook out the sheet and handed him one corner. "I'll help you."

The sheet billowed as they each grabbed an end, and some flowery scent wafted into the air. They secured it around the edges of the couch and Judd tossed the pillow onto one end.

"Perfect." He poked a few buttons on his watch. "What time is your meeting tomorrow morning? I'll need to go home first and change, and then I'll meet you in the lobby of your office building."

"Do you know where it's located?"

"I did some research on you after I left today."

Her eyebrows jumped. "Did you discover anything interesting?"

"Let's see." He raised his eyes to the ceiling. "Lots of crazy parties, wild friends, escape from boarding school, a few arrests, exotic travel. Typical life of an idle rich girl."

"Ouch." She clamped her hands over her stomach as if he'd stabbed her.

"Hey, no judgment here." He turned off the lamp beside the couch. "Get some sleep, London."

She crept away in the darkness and turned at the bottom of the stairs. Her whisper floated across the room. "I'm changing all that."

Before he could reply that it didn't concern him one way or the other, she'd jogged upstairs, and a door slammed in the recesses of the condo.

Probably a good thing he hadn't had time to answer. She seemed sensitive about her wild-child image. And besides, he would've been lying—it did concern him.

Everything about London Breck concerned him.

JUDD ROLLED UP his motorcycle jacket and stuffed it into one of his bike's saddlebags. Leaning forward, he ran one hand through his helmet hair and then tugged on the lapels of his suit jacket.

Sean had helped him pick out the suit. As fastidious about his clothes as he was about everything else in his life, his brother knew a good suit and a good tailor. Judd felt at ease that he'd fit in with any of these financial types at Breck Global Enterprises.

He ambled from the parking garage into the lobby of the building where BGE occupied the top four floors. He parked himself next to a potted plant and watched the twirling glass doors from the street to the lobby.

A tall, cool blonde with her hair in a loose bun sailed through the doors. London shoved her sunglasses on top of her head and hoisted the soft-sided black briefcase over her shoulder.

When Judd stepped into her path, a hitch hampered her long stride but didn't stop her. He matched her step for step on the way to the elevator.

She pressed the button and cranked her head to the side,

her gaze scanning him head to toe. "Nice suit. You look like Secret Service with those sunglasses."

He took them off and slipped them into his front pocket. "Better?"

"How'd you sleep last night? I didn't think you'd be gone when I got up."

His pulse quickened. "Everything okay this morning?"

"Fine." She stabbed the button again. "So were the accommodations satisfactory?"

"Fine." He'd slept lightly. A few bumps in the night had had him bolting upright, but he'd put them down to the settling of the building.

A few other people joined them in the elevator.

London shifted toward him, close enough for him to see the sparkle from the dusting of powder across her nose.

"Here's the agenda for the morning. I'll look over my email and return any calls. The meeting starts at nine o'clock. I'll try to point out all the players to you beforehand, and maybe you can hang out in my office during the meeting and go through some company files."

"Sounds good."

The doors to the elevator swished open, and Judd stepped back and held the door for the others. Silence reigned as the car delivered the other three to their destinations.

When the doors closed behind the last person, London turned to him. "If anyone asks, you're just additional security."

"Got it." He saluted. "Nice to meet you, I'm additional security."

She drummed her fingers against his biceps. "Very funny. Did you hear anything more about Griff? Is it in the paper?"

"I haven't heard anything, and I didn't see it in the newspaper, but it's probably online."

"I know nothing." She traced her fingertip along the seam of her lips.

Sleeping downstairs last night had been the best move he could've made. This woman, with her hard shell on the outside and squishy, soft insides, had gotten under his skin. Her reputation as a hot party chick had hooked him, but her wit and self-deprecating humor were reeling him in.

The elevator took them to the very top of the building and spit them out onto plush carpet, facing a glass-block wall with the BGE logo shimmering on it.

London exited to the right and he followed her to a reception area adorned with fine art, a couple of chairs, a few exotic plants and an even more exotic receptionist behind a mahogany desk.

"Good morning, Arianna." London flashed a smile at the receptionist, who could moonlight as a model.

"Good morning, London." Her dark eyes flicked to Judd.

"This is Judd Brody. He's going to be providing some extra personal security for me in the next few months."

Months? He had to maintain a professional demeanor with this woman for months?

He nodded toward Arianna, who smiled serenely, as if a personal bodyguard was the most common accoutrement in the world.

London continued to the back of the building, where individual offices lined the walls and buzzing office staffers guarded their ground.

London nodded and waved her way through the maze until she reached the back office. Another impeccably coiffed and dressed woman sat with perfect posture behind a desk.

"Good morning, London."

"Good morning, Celine. Everything ready for the meeting this morning?"

Celine's gaze darted toward Judd and back to London's face. "All on your desk. Roger has already been by this morning."

"Thanks." She tilted her chin at him. "This is Judd Brody. He's…uh, with security."

Celine smiled brightly. "Good morning. Would either of you like some coffee?"

"I would. Judd?"

"Black."

Celine scooted back from her chair and scurried out the door.

An older gentleman—silver hair, impeccable suit, moneyed ease—strolled into the outer office. "Nice to see you here, London. Are you ready for the meeting?"

"I am."

"I'll be seated to your right, and I can guide you through anything that throws you for a loop."

"Thanks, Richard." She made a half turn toward Judd. "Richard, this is Judd Brody. He'll be providing some additional personal security for me. Judd, Richard Taylor, executive vice president of BGE."

Richard nodded, a tight smile on his patrician face. "Welcome aboard."

Richard must have thought Judd was a new BGE employee or something, but if London didn't see fit to correct him, far be it from Judd to do so. He nodded back.

Did the vice president have a hankering to be CEO?

"I'll see you at the meeting, London—nine sharp." He pivoted out of the room, almost colliding with Celine carrying two cups of coffee.

"Sorry, Mr. Taylor." Celine rolled her eyes at London and handed them the coffee.

London waved Judd through another door. "My office." She shut the door behind them and sighed. "You don't know how much I hate walking through that gauntlet of employees."

"Why?"

"I don't know. They all work for me. Their livelihoods depend on me and my decisions. I feel like they're out there sizing me up."

"They probably are." He perched on the edge of her desk and folded his arms. "Why does my job title keep changing for every person I meet?"

"They're all the same, aren't they?" She dropped her briefcase on the floor by her chair.

"It all sounds vague."

"I don't know." She eased into the big leather chair behind the desk. "You want me to keep quiet about the threats, and I don't want to come across as paranoid."

"What's the saying? If someone really is trying to get you, it's not paranoia."

Tapping the keyboard of her desktop computer, she said, "I thought I wasn't giving anyone the full scoop."

"Might be fun just to see their reactions. I wonder if anything could break the mask that Richard Taylor wears. He's one smooth SOB, isn't he?"

"Always has been. Do you want to meet the rest of the likely suspects?" She twisted her monitor to one side. "I've got the rogues' gallery right here."

He stepped around to the other side of the desk and leaned over her shoulder, taking in a webpage with an org chart and photos. He tapped a finger on the top picture— Spencer Breck. "Looks like it needs to be updated."

"Putting my picture up there will make it seem so final." She scooted her chair to the side. "Have a seat."

He pulled a heavy chair as close to the desk as he could get it and hunched over.

She rattled off names and positions. He'd have to print out this chart and study it more closely, maybe do a little background on these people.

He held up his hand when she got to her cousin Niles. "Tell me about him."

"He's not much for business but loves the trappings. My father and his had their issues, and Dad never much liked Niles. Left him some money and property in his trust, but not much responsibility at BGE."

"Is Niles an only child, too?"

"Too?"

"Like you."

"I thought I told you at the bar, I'm not an only child." Her finger drew a circle around the picture of a serious-looking dark-haired man in his mid-thirties. "That's my half brother, Wade."

"You did mention a half brother." Judd squinted at the name beneath the picture. "Wade Vickers. He's not a Breck?"

"Vickers is his mother's name. He never took the Breck name."

"Bad blood between his mother and your father?"

"You could say that. Wade was born before my parents married, so my father could've married Wade's mother. He didn't."

"But your father still gave him a place in the company."

"No reason not to." She shrugged. "He's smart, has a good head for business and likes this stuff a lot more than I do."

"Your father still left you in charge."

"Go figure."

Wedging a knuckle beneath her chin, he turned her face toward his. "Why are you here, London?"

"Because my father left me in charge, and I have something to prove." Her bottom lip trembled. "It was his last ditch effort to…to…"

"Turn you into him?" He waved his hand around the

office with its gleaming surfaces and dark leather. "This is him, not you."

She wrinkled her nose as she glanced around the room. "I plan to redecorate."

"I'm not talking about the decor. I mean all of it—the corporate world, shareholder meetings, the bottom line."

"This *is* me." She jumped up from her chair and smacked her palms on the desk. "I can do this. You don't know anything. You don't know me, Judd Brody. I'm not that girl in the tabloids. Not anymore."

She was right. What made him think he could give her advice, judge her? And why did he care?

"Okay, okay." He shrugged his shoulders. "Maybe this is you. What the hell do I know?"

"Let's get back to what you do know. Anything about any of these guys that jumps out at you? Honestly, I can't imagine any of them going to such lengths to threaten me. A few of them have told me straight up I'm in over my head and to give it up—sort of like you."

"Wait a minute. I never said that. You can probably do whatever you set your mind to. I just didn't think the corporate world was a good fit for you, but you set me straight." He steepled his fingers. "Any one of them has motive enough for getting rid of you, I suppose. How do you and your brother get along?"

Walking to the front of her desk, she smoothed back a piece of hair that had slipped out of the bun—another affectation. The bun didn't suit her, either.

"Wade is more like my father than I am. He's almost ten years older than I am—wife, couple of kids. He's a good guy, if a little dull."

He took in the four walls of the office. This environment could make anyone dull. "You two are on friendly terms?"

"I'd say so."

"Did your father take care of him in his will? Is your brother satisfied working for you?"

"Wade is very comfortable, thanks to Dad, and he's happy with his numbers." She sighed and perched on the edge of the desk. "I wish there was one villain to point to, but BGE has no villains."

The door to her office burst open and a stocky man with dark hair charged through, with Celine on his heels. "I asked him to wait, London."

The guy bounded across the room, landed in front of London, grabbed her shoulders and planted a kiss on her mouth. "La-La, I missed you so much. I came straight here from the airport."

Judd rose from his chair, his hands curling into fists. Who was this guy and who the hell was La-La?

"London?"

She turned a flushed face toward Judd, her hands against the man's chest.

The intruder glanced at Judd as if seeing him for the first time and raised one eyebrow. "Who's this?"

Judd expanded his chest and took one step forward. "Who the hell are you?"

The man finally dropped his hands from London's shoulders and turned to face Judd fully. "I'm London's fiancé."

Chapter Seven

London rolled her eyes. *Here we go again.*

She'd better say something, since Judd looked about ready to use Roger for a punching bag and Roger looked about ready to slap Judd across the face with a glove.

She sliced a hand between the two men. "Not exactly, Roger."

"You mean, not yet." He chucked her under the chin with his knuckle, a gesture similar to one Judd had used on her just a moment ago. Only when Roger did it, she felt about two years old.

"Roger, this is Judd Brody. I hired him for some additional personal security. Judd, this is Roger Taylor, CFO of Breck Global and Richard's son."

Judd thrust out his hand. "Sorry about the earlier antagonism. Ms. Breck never mentioned her engagement to me, so when a strange man burst in here and grabbed her, my adrenaline started to pump."

Roger eyed the tattoos peeking from the sleeve of Judd's jacket. "No worries. London could use a little extra security, but you're not from BGE, are you? Unless you joined the staff while I was out of the country."

"He did." She met Judd's gaze over Roger's shoulder and put a finger to her lips. It would make her life easier if Roger didn't know she didn't trust BGE security—at least not with her life. She just needed to stick with the same story for everyone.

Judd dipped his head. "New hire."

London let out a measured breath. "I'll see you in the boardroom, Roger. Judd and I have a few things to review."

Roger reached for her again, but this time she side-stepped him. She didn't want him mauling her, especially under Judd's watchful glare.

Roger winked and turned his fingers into a gun, pointing at her. "Don't you worry about a thing, London. I'll be right there beside you in the boardroom."

She pasted a smile on her face and nodded.

Roger exited the office, calling out to Celine, "Grab me a coffee."

London snapped the door closed and rested her forehead against the heavy wood. "Now I have to smooth Celine's feathers since she absolutely hates it when Roger orders her around. He has his own executive assistant."

"Fiancé?"

"No." She turned, putting her hands behind her back and pressing them against the door. "He likes to think we have some understanding, but we don't. I don't. We dated a few times over the years, but we are not compatible in any way."

"I can't imagine how a guy like that with a stick up his... back could ever think he'd be happy with a woman with your wild ways."

She opened her mouth and Judd held up his hand. "Former wild ways."

"That's just it." She blew a strand of hair from her face for about the hundredth time that morning. "He loves my former wild ways. He used to pretend my antics frustrated him, but that was an act. My mishaps allowed him to be paternal toward me, correcting and chastising me."

"That sounds like a seriously creepy dynamic."

"Part of it has to do with all this." She spread her arms

wide. "If I keep screwing up, it gives him greater control over me and BGE—at least he thinks so."

"Does he want it enough to kill for it?"

"Roger? I don't see him as a killer, but he wants it enough to marry me for it."

Judd's blue eyes glittered, almost slicing through her. "And that would be a great hardship for him?"

The warmth started in her belly and made a fast approach to her face. She snorted and made a beeline to her desk, ducking into one of the drawers. "For him, I think it would be, but I'm going to spare him the sacrifice."

She retrieved a pad of paper from the drawer and smacked it on the desk. "You can work in here while I attend the meeting."

"How long will you be?"

"About two hours." She couldn't stop the grimace that twisted her lips. "Then I'm going to stop by the hospital and visit Theodore. Do you want to come along?"

"Absolutely. I'm your bodyguard, remember?"

When he looked the way he did now, his raw power barely contained by his suit and his eyes hard and... possessive, she didn't want to forget.

She'd hardly gotten one wink of sleep last night with him downstairs on her couch. She could understand he wanted to keep their relationship professional. He must have all his female clients throwing themselves at him, and he couldn't accept every offer.

Hell, if he made good on the promise in his eyes, she'd be wondering if he bodyguarded everyone the same way.

Celine's tap on the door broke the spell between them.

"C'mon in."

"Meeting in ten minutes. You probably want to be one of the first people there."

"Thanks, Celine. Sorry about Roger."

"He's so annoying."

"I know. I'll talk to him again." She gestured to Judd, who had removed his suit jacket and draped it over the back of a chair. "Judd's going to be working in my office while I'm in the meeting. After the meeting, I'm leaving for the rest of the day."

Celine's eyes widened behind her trendy glasses as she took in the view of Judd stretching, his muscles shifting beneath his crisp white shirt. She swallowed. "Okay. Let me know if you need anything, Judd—more coffee, water, supplies."

A back rub. A soft place to rest your head. A mother for your children.

The thoughts marching across Celine's face could be London's own.

London dipped behind the desk and grabbed her briefcase. Might as well look as though she knew what she was doing, even if she was clueless.

Judd looked up, oblivious to the drooling females before him. "Knock 'em dead."

London reached back, plucking the pins from her hair and shaking it free from the bun. "I will."

JUDD RUBBED HIS eyes and shifted his chair to take in the view out the window. Spectacular. It still couldn't make up for being ensconced in an office in a suit all morning.

The job of CEO of an international corporation did not suit London—and it had nothing to do with her intelligence, her ability or her crazy ways. Maybe a little to do with her crazy ways. She struck him as a free spirit. This job might as well have *free spirits need not apply* stamped across its letterhead.

What had a hardheaded businessman like Spencer Breck been thinking when he'd left control of the company to her? Maybe he'd done it for spite.

Maybe father and daughter never got along. She hadn't

seemed all that broken up over his death. Of course, what gave him any idea that he could adequately judge grief? He'd stuffed his away for years.

His brothers had been stoked when the real Phone Book Killer had revealed himself, but the news had left him empty—as usual. His old man had still offed himself. What kind of man did that to his family?

From all accounts, his father had been a good detective. When the Phone Book Killer had started his killing spree, the killer had begun sending messages to Detective Joseph Brody. The SFPD brass had become suspicious about the messages, and then evidence linking his father to the crimes turned up. His father was innocent, so why didn't he stick around and fight for justice instead of ending it all with a jump from the Golden Gate Bridge?

Celine knocked on the door for the tenth time in an hour, and he invited her in. This time she had company.

"Judd? Sorry to bother you again, but we need to leave something on London's desk."

The older woman with Celine scowled at him over her glasses, her gray eyebrows meeting over her nose. "Who are you?"

Celine's cheeks sported two red circles. "I told you, Mary. He's working for London."

Mary's gaze traveled from Judd's face to his arms, which were bared to the elbow. "As what?"

Celine giggled and rolled her eyes. "He's in security."

The woman turned, blocking Celine's entrance. "That's all, Celine. I'll take it from here."

Shooting him a glance over the ogre's shoulder, Celine backed out of the room.

When the door closed, Mary broadened her stance and crossed her arms over her ample bosom. "BGE security working alone in the boss's office?"

Judd kicked his feet on top of London's desk and crossed

his arms behind his head. "Celine forgot her manners. Who are you and what do you want to leave for London?"

"You're a smooth operator, aren't you?" She pulled back her shoulders and Judd feared the buttons on her high-necked white blouse would pop. "My name is Mary Kowalski, and I was Mr. Breck's secretary for forty years. None of this administrative assistant nonsense. I wasn't Mr. Breck's assistant. I was his secretary—I took shorthand, typed one hundred words a minute and, yes, I got him coffee and picked up his dry cleaning, because that's what we did back when I was first hired, and I was grateful for the job. I maintained the same level of service until the day I retired."

Judd's eyebrows had been rising with each of Mary's words, so they were probably somewhere on the back of his skull by now.

He removed his feet from the desk and rose, Mary's eyes following his ascent. "Nice to meet you, ma'am. I'm Judd Brody, and Ms. Breck hired me as her personal bodyguard."

"You're a big 'un, aren't you? That's handy in a bodyguard." She reached into her enormous handbag and drew out a white envelope. She shook it at him. "You're one of those Brody boys. I followed your father's case closely. He'd been a good cop for years. I knew Detective Brody was no killer."

"That I am, ma'am."

"You can stop with the *ma'am* nonsense. Call me Mary and I'll call you Judd." She settled herself in the chair facing the desk. "How's our girl doing?"

"Our girl?"

"London." She chuckled. "Is she stepping in it yet with those ridiculous heels she favors?"

"Stepping in it?"

"Are you a P.I. or a parrot?"

He choked and took a swig of water. "I think she's doing just fine."

"Nonsense. She's not cut out for this. I don't know what Mr. Breck was thinking."

Since that was exactly what he'd been wondering, he warmed up to Mary even more, although she reminded him of his first-grade teacher, Mrs. K. Treated him like Mrs. K. had treated him, too.

"She's a grown woman. I suppose she can make her own decisions. I'm just here to—" he closed the website on the monitor "—make sure she's safe."

"All kinds of ways to make sure someone's safe. I heard someone beat up Theodore two nights ago."

She must not have heard about Griff. "He's in the hospital."

She scowled and placed the envelope she'd had in her lap between a pencil holder and a framed photograph— one of Spencer Breck shaking the hand of some guy in a uniform as he got an award.

"Then London did the right thing hiring you. The first sensible thing she's done since her father died."

"Were London and her father close?"

She smoothed her hands over her skirt. "She wouldn't say so, but he loved and admired his girl."

"Admired?" That seemed to be an odd sentiment for a father to have about his daughter. Should be the other way around. Not that he admired his father—not at all.

Mary shifted her eyes from his face to just over his shoulder. "He admired her honesty and that she had the guts to do just what she wanted to do. It's only when she tries to please someone else that she gets confused." Her eyes found his again. "Like now."

He couldn't agree more, but he didn't think anyone could dissuade London from taking control of BGE—not even a killer.

Glancing at his watch, he said, "She should be back soon. Do you want to wait for her?"

"No." She struggled to her feet from the deep leather chair, and Judd rushed around the desk to help her. She tapped the edge of the envelope with her finger. "I just came to bring her that."

"Will she know what it is?"

"I don't even know what it is." She kept hold of his arm with one hand while she tugged at her skirt with the other. "It's from her father. He gave it to me two years ago and asked me to deliver it to London a few months after his death."

"Maybe it's the reprieve she's been looking for, and he's rescinding his offer of the company."

"I wish." Mary drummed her chin with her fingertips. "Anyway, when I retired last year, I asked Mr. Breck if he still wanted me to hang on to the envelope, and he did. Same instructions. If I'd passed away first, I assumed he would've given the same instructions to someone else."

"Mary!" London barreled into the room and practically tackled the older woman. She wrapped her in a bear hug. "What are you doing here? Can I convince you to come out of retirement and come back to work?"

Mary smiled for the first time since entering the office as she stroked London's hair back from her face. "You look good, a little tired."

"The past few days have been crazy." She raised an eyebrow at Judd. "Have you met Judd Brody?"

"We were discussing you." She broke away from London and grabbed his biceps, giving it a squeeze. "You let this man look out for you. I get a good feeling from this one."

"That's what he's doing here, but what about you? What brings you to BGE?"

"I brought you something." Mary pointed to the envelope on the desk. "From your father."

"More forms?"

"I don't know what it is, London. He gave it to me a

few years ago with instructions to hand it off to you after he passed."

"That sounds mysterious. Why wouldn't he just give it to his attorney?"

Mary clicked her tongue. "You know I never asked your father questions. Not my place."

London reached for the envelope, and Mary crossed two fingers in front of her. "Don't open it while I'm here. It's a private matter and you need to keep it private."

London dropped the envelope. "I'll wait. Can I buy you lunch?"

"Does it look like I need lunch?" Mary patted her belly. "I'm meeting my walking group at the wharf today."

"That's great, Mary."

"It's not so great, but it keeps my doctor happy." She leveled a finger at Judd. "You take care of her, Judd Brody. She deserves the moon and the stars."

London walked Mary out of the office into the outer area, where it looked as if Mary was giving Celine a few parting instructions.

London returned to the office laughing; that little vertical line that had been in place when she'd returned from the meeting had disappeared. "Mary is a character. Did she scare you?"

"Took me back to first grade."

She tilted her head to one side. "I can't see you as a first grader. Shy loner?"

"Close—class clown." He kicked out the chair Mary had just vacated. "How'd the meeting go?"

"Boring and largely incomprehensible." She sank into the chair and then straightened her spine. "But really informative. I learned a lot."

He flicked the envelope with his fingers. "Are you going to open this message from your father?"

"I thought the old man was dead."

Judd glanced up at the open door to see London's cousin gripping the doorjamb.

London twisted in her chair. "Something more from the meeting, Niles?"

"No. Just heard the scuttlebutt about your new bodyguard and came to see for myself."

"This is Judd Brody. Judd, this is my cousin, Niles Breck."

Judd nodded but didn't rise. London didn't have to introduce him around as if he was her date.

"I'm glad you're watching my feckless cousin, but why do you need more security, London? Bunny told me what happened to you in the alley. I've told you before to use the front entrances and brave the paparazzi. At least they're not out to snatch your priceless jewels."

"There have been a couple of incidents. Anyway, his salary is not coming out of your pocket, so don't worry about it."

"What did I hear when I walked in? You got a message from your father? How did he manage that?"

A tall man came up behind Niles and tapped him on the shoulder. "Do you have those figures for me?"

"Did you come to check out the new guy in security, too, Wade?"

London's brother, tall and thin like his cousins, pursed his lips. "I did not, although I don't think it's a bad idea."

"Brody." Niles snapped his fingers. "Your brother is a homicide detective and your father—"

"That's right." Judd crossed his arms.

Wade's detached demeanor sharpened at Niles's announcement, but he backed out of the office, nudging Niles. "Those figures?"

"Duty calls." He tugged at the narrow lapels of his suit. "I'll leave you with that message from beyond the grave."

The door closed behind the two men and Judd let out a breath.

"You did call it a message." She lunged for the envelope. "I just figured it was another form or document that I have to sign—one in a tall stack of many."

"I don't know what it is, London. I can hit the men's room if you want to read it in privacy."

"Oh." She fanned herself with the envelope. "If you think it's some sentimental missive from dear old Dad, you can relax. He did not roll that way."

"Okay, then, I'm going to close out of this stuff I was going through, and we can get going—unless you need to handle anything from the meeting."

"Nope. It's all being handled by other people. Other people can do this. Other people can do that." She slipped her finger into the fold of the envelope and ripped across.

Judd hunched over the computer and closed some files. London had been chattering, and then she fell silent.

He looked up. Her eyes were huge glassy pools in her pale face.

"What's wrong?" He almost leaped across the desk, but her accusing tone stopped him.

"Is this some kind of joke?"

His fingers, wedged against the desk, curled into the wood. "What are you talking about?"

"This." She waved a single sheet of paper at him. "Is this your idea of a joke?"

"London, I don't know what you're talking about."

She flung the paper at him; it settled on the keyboard.

He picked it up by one corner and read it aloud. "'Detective Joseph Brody is innocent of murder. At least tell his sons that. They deserve to know.'"

The paper slipped from his fingers, and the room tilted.

What the hell did his father have to do with Spencer Breck?

Chapter Eight

London blinked. Judd looked as dazed as she felt.

What did it mean? Why was her father's last communication to her about Joseph Brody? And what were the odds that one of Joseph Brody's sons would be standing right across from her while she received it?

"Y-you don't know anything about this?"

He fell heavily into the chair and plowed his fingers through his thick hair. "What do you mean? Know anything about it as if I wrote it and sent it? Is that what you think? Mary brought it. I never saw this note before in my life and I don't have a clue what your father knows about my father and why he'd tell you anything about it."

"This is crazy." She massaged her temples. "Why would he send me this note about your father after his death?"

"Could it be someone else playing a joke?"

"What kind of joke is this?"

"You tell me, since you just accused me of playing it on you."

"Why would my father want to tell me this? And why didn't he just tell me while he was alive?"

"Did he ever mention the Phone Book Killer case or my father?"

"Not that I recall. Maybe he had some contact with your brother? The detective? He was a big supporter of the SFPD.

He was close to Captain Williams. He was even on the police commission at one time."

Judd leaned over in his chair and plucked the piece of paper up from the carpet where it had drifted. He smoothed it out on the desk. "I have no idea if he ever contacted Sean, but I intend to ask him."

"My dad died before your other brother, Eric, uncovered the truth about the Phone Book Killer. Maybe if he had lived to see that day, he would've gotten rid of this note. But why write it in the first place? It's a crazy coincidence that I hired one of Joseph Brody's sons to protect me. Maybe Dad was guiding me the night of the benefit."

"Do you believe that kind of stuff? My future sister-in-law is…sensitive that way."

"Yes, I heard. She was involved in catching that occult serial killer after he kidnapped her daughter." She gripped her upper arms and shivered.

"How far back was your father involved with the department?"

"Way far back, when my mother was still alive. There are some pictures at his house showing him and my mother at some police functions." She snatched the picture on the desk and tapped it. "This is my father and Captain Williams."

"Did the support start over twenty years ago?"

"Definitely. Is that when your father—"

"Yeah." The line of his jaw hardened. "The note exonerates my father as the Phone Book Killer, but it doesn't explain why he jumped from the bridge."

It always came back to that for Judd. He'd never be able to forgive his father. They had that in common.

"This is one of those freaky coincidences, or maybe your FBI sister-in-law is right—there are mysterious forces at work in the universe."

"Those mysterious forces still don't explain how your

father knew mine was innocent, and why he thought it was so important for you to impart this info to me and my brothers."

"Maybe Mary knows." She snapped her fingers. "Maybe Theodore knows. He was with my father almost as long as Mary was."

"Then let's pay a visit to Theodore."

A half an hour later, London tapped the toe of her shoe on the sidewalk as she watched Judd climb off his bike and secure his helmet to the side. The incongruity of the suit and the Harley only made Judd look hotter. If she hadn't been wearing this straight skirt, she would've climbed on the back again.

That had been the best part of these past few days— riding on the back of Judd's Harley. Actually, Judd had been the best part of these past few days—the past few months.

After reading her father's note, she had to believe the stars had fated her meeting with Judd the other night. He'd been with her when Theodore was attacked and when she'd discovered her ransacked home. He ran a hand through his hair and straightened his suit jacket. He didn't look much like a guardian angel, but he'd come through for her twice.

"How'd your taxi get here so fast?" The hospital doors slid open and Judd waved her through first.

"I think he figured the faster he went the better tip he'd get."

"Did it work?"

"I'm a big tipper anyway. Last thing you want as a rich person is to get the reputation of a cheap tipper."

"I'll remember that about rich people."

"Some of them don't care. There are plenty of chintzy tippers among the rich."

"I'll remember that, too." He stabbed the elevator button. "You're giving me a lot of good information about rich people."

"Ha." She smacked the button for good measure. "I have a feeling you've been in contact with a lot of rich people in your line of work."

"Yeah, but none have ever divulged the secrets of the rich to me before."

The elevator doors opened and she stepped into the car. "I know. I talk too much."

"You're the most normal rich person I've ever met. So there's that."

She tossed back her hair and laughed. "Yeah, we're a strange bunch."

"Nice to hear you laugh." He cocked his head. "Does that mean you've dismissed the idea that I somehow engineered that note from your father?"

"I didn't think that."

"Yeah, you did. You said it with your eyes and the tone of your voice. You thought I'd tricked you in some way."

She smoothed her hand across her warm cheek. "The note surprised me, shocked me."

"That's another thing about most rich people."

"What's that?"

The doors opened and Judd smacked his hand against one side. "You always have to worry about people using you."

She walked past him quickly, tears stinging the backs of her eyes. She'd exposed her weaknesses to him and must seem pathetic in his eyes. She shrugged. "Poor little rich girl should walk a mile in someone else's shoes, where the fear of feeding your family trumps the fear of being used for your money."

"Hey." Judd grabbed her arm. "I never said that. We all have our problems—rich and poor."

Now he felt he had to make her feel better? She stopped in front of Theodore's room. "And Theodore has his problems."

When they pushed through the door, a young woman

sprang up from the chair beside Theodore's bed. "You must be London Breck."

"And you must be Shannon." She reached out and took Theodore's daughter's hand. "I'm so sorry this happened to your dad."

"Dad's an ex-marine. He had no intention of backing off when those men tried to steal the car."

Theodore grunted. "Those fellas messed with the wrong driver."

London studied Theodore's bruised face. "You're looking a little better."

Theodore grunted again. "Time to get out of this place. The food alone will kill you."

London made a half turn toward Judd. "Shannon, this is Judd Brody."

Shannon grabbed Judd's hand in both of hers. "Thank you so much. Dad told me you probably saved his life when you attended to him in that bar."

"I wouldn't go that far. The paramedics got there fast."

"I owe you one, Brody." Theodore winced and sank against his pillows.

"And I owe you, London." Shannon flung her arm to the side. "Dad's insurance doesn't cover this private room or the extra day he's been in here. The nurses' station out front said it had been taken care of, and I'm sure that means you."

"Your father works for BGE and he's been a family friend for years." London gripped the back of the plastic chair and leaned over it.

"Well, I appreciate it, and my sister and I appreciate that you called us right away."

"I'm just glad you could come on such short notice. That's another thing, and I don't want any arguments. I'm paying your expenses."

Shannon opened her mouth, but London stopped her with an upheld hand. If she couldn't do stuff like this with all the money she had, what was the point in having it? "It's done. Now, why don't you go get something to eat while I talk to your dad?"

Shannon's gaze traveled to Theodore, who waved his hand. "Go on, girl. I'm mighty tired of your fussing."

Shannon wedged her hands on her hips. "You can have him, London."

When Shannon closed the door, London skirted the chair and sat down. "Are you feeling better, Theodore?"

"Don't you start. I feel fine."

"Good." She pulled the envelope from her purse. "I have something to ask you about Dad."

His eyes dropped to the envelope. "Fire away."

"Did Dad ever say anything to you about Joseph Brody and the Phone Book Killer case?" If she expected surprise on Theodore's face, he didn't deliver. Her pulse ticked up a notch. "Did he?"

Theodore looked at Judd. "He knew about it—everyone did. He was even on the police commission at the time."

"He was?" She scooted her chair closer. "What did he say about it then?"

"When some of that evidence came out against Brody—" Theodore's eyes shifted to Judd again "—he was surprised, like everyone else. Thought it was…unfortunate that a good detective had fooled everyone. Thought it was an embarrassment for the department."

Judd braced one shoulder against the wall. "He believed in my father's guilt?"

"At the time I think he got caught up in it, but it turned out that first victim's husband was just trying to cover his tracks."

London twisted the edge of the bedsheets. "We know that now, but are you telling us that Dad believed Joseph Brody was the Phone Book Killer?"

"He did. Sorry, man."

Judd pushed off the wall. "No offense taken. A lot of people thought he was guilty. He killed himself—that sort of screams guilt."

"That's weird." She pulled the note from the envelope. "At one point, did Dad change his mind, and why?" She shook out the note and handed it to Theodore. "Looks as though he felt bad about it and wanted to somehow set the record straight."

Theodore reached for his glasses on the bedside cart and put them on. He held up the note and scanned it. "Where'd you find this?"

"That's what's so strange. Mary Kowalski hand delivered it to me. Said Dad asked her to keep it and give it to me after he died."

Theodore's forehead furrowed. "That doesn't make any sense."

"Exactly. I thought you might be able to shed some light on it, but you've only added to the mystery."

"Not really." Judd shoved off the wall and loomed over Theodore's bed. "You said he was on the police commission at the time. Who else was on the commission?"

"Couldn't tell you that, but I'm sure you could find out. What are you aiming at?"

"I'm not sure. If he knew my father was innocent, maybe others on the commission knew it, too." Judd blew out a breath and stepped back. "You know what? It doesn't really matter, does it? The real killer confessed to my brother, and my father's name has been cleared. How or why your father knew about it isn't an issue at this point, is it?"

London narrowed her eyes. For a minute there, Judd had dropped the pretense of not giving a hoot about his father's reputation, but he'd recovered himself nicely—back to the aloof, slightly sardonic, devil-may-care P.I.

"I just think it's weird that my father left me a note from the grave about this. Why not some warm words for me or remembrances of my mother? It's clearly something that bothered him."

"Now your father's dead, my father's dead and his name has been cleared." Judd's heavy lids fell over his eyes. "Doesn't matter."

Theodore nodded. "I agree, London."

"I guess I've been overruled here." She snatched the letter from Theodore's lap and stuffed it back in the envelope. "Are you going back to Atlanta to see your other daughter when you get out of here? I know you have another grandson you haven't seen yet."

"I know that tone of voice." He rolled his eyes at Judd and winked. "Boss's orders?"

"Boss's orders." London's lips twitched. Sometimes it was good to be the boss. "Let me know before you leave town. Call me at the office—something happened to my phone."

She heard Judd's intake of breath but ignored him. She didn't want to tell Theodore about the break-in at her place or Griff's murder. He might get it into his head to stick around.

She had all the bodyguard she needed.

"I'll do that. If they let me out of here tomorrow, I'll probably take a few days to make arrangements before leaving."

"Make sure you put all expenses on your BGE credit card—airfare, everything. I mean it."

"Yes, ma'am."

They waited until Shannon returned before leaving Theodore.

Judd turned to her at the elevator. "You didn't want to tell him what happened at your place?"

"I didn't want to worry him."

"I agree. Nothing he could do about it anyway."

They reached the lobby and Judd hesitated at the door. "Are you going straight back to your place?"

"Yeah." She patted her stomach. "We never did have lunch."

"I could use something to eat. I was going to stop by my office and get that equipment I mentioned yesterday. I still want to do a clean sweep for bugs at your place."

"Why don't you do that, and we'll meet at a restaurant near your office for lunch. I can grab a taxi over."

"There's a decent Italian place down the block from my place—Napoli's."

"I know it. I'll get us a table."

She snagged a taxi near the emergency room entrance as Judd took off on his bike. She gave the driver her location and collapsed in the backseat. Both Theodore and Judd had been quick to dismiss her father's note, but she couldn't do it. She and her father hadn't always gotten along, but she knew him. For him to leave a note with Mary to give to her after his death, it had to be something of great importance.

Why hadn't he told her this when he was alive? Better yet, why not tell the Brodys? If he felt so bad about it, why not tell the people it affected the most?

The police commission. It had to be related to his time on the commission. It coincided with the events of Detective Brody's downfall. Maybe unraveling this mystery would help reveal the reason behind Brody's suicide.

That alone should motivate Judd. The fact that his father had taken his life bothered him more than the suspicions surrounding Joseph Brody. Maybe she could use her pull to give Judd some closure on the issue. That would be worth more than any retainer she could pay him.

"Excuse me." She leaned forward in her seat. "I need to make a stop first. Take me to the financial district."

The taxi driver nodded and took the next turn.

When he pulled up in front of the building, she said,

"Wait here. I'll be about ten minutes." She dashed into the building and back up to the BGE offices.

When she saw London, Celine reddened up to the roots of her hair and jumped off the edge of her desk, where she'd been flirting with one of the guys from marketing. "Did you forget something, London?"

"Yeah, in my office." She brushed her fingers in Celine's direction as she started for the office. "I'll get it."

London closed the door behind her and pressed a button to drop the blinds over the windows. She moved behind the desk and extended her foot beneath it to feel for the lump beneath the carpet. When she located it, she pressed down with her foot.

She ducked under the desk and lifted a piece of carpet. Then she slid a panel of the floor to the side and reached in for her father's laptop.

When he'd showed her this hiding place, he'd told her that nobody knew about it, not even Mary.

She'd seen him put this laptop in here before and hadn't thought about it when he'd passed away, since all the main BGE business resided on the desktop computer in this office. But this had been his private laptop, and if her father had had any secrets they would be on this computer.

Just like she'd kept her secrets on her laptop—the one that had been stolen from her place yesterday morning.

Maybe her father had had the right idea with a secret hiding place.

She replaced the panel and carpet and then smoothed it with her hand. She shoved the laptop into her briefcase.

Leaving the blinds closed, she swung the door open.

Celine had returned to her chair and was typing away on her keyboard. "Did you find everything okay?"

"I did, thanks." She slowed her gait. "I forgot to mention that I'm going to get a new phone. I don't have mine anymore."

Celine stopped typing and shoved her glasses onto her nose. "London, is it true that a security guard at your building was murdered last night and that you found his body?"

London stumbled to a stop. Did everyone know the rest of the story? "Yes, I did. The police don't want me to say anything about it right now."

"That's so creepy. Is that why you have tall, dark and gorgeous looking out for you?"

"A little extra security never hurt anyone."

"Especially extra security like Judd Brody. He can guard my body anytime."

London had no idea what kind of expression just crossed her face, but it had Celine backpedaling. "I—I mean, I'm sure he's professional and all and you don't see him like that. And I don't see him like—or I wouldn't see him like that if he was guarding my body...I mean, if he was my bodyguard."

London tried a stiff smile. "I know what you mean. He's a good-looking man."

"Well, have a great day." Celine waved and dipped her head toward her monitor again.

London traipsed toward the elevator, the added weight of the laptop causing her briefcase to bang against her hip. She'd probably just confirmed to Celine that she thought of Judd as much more than a bodyguard. Maybe she never should've invited Celine to call her London. Mary still called her father Mr. Breck, even after his death.

She could be a different kind of CEO than her father and still be successful, couldn't she? Of course, she didn't even know what a successful CEO looked like. Did it mean having everyone around you address you by your surname?

Too bad her father hadn't left her a rule book—*Being a CEO for Dummies*.

She scrambled back into the taxi. "Okay, on to Napoli's."

She still beat Judd to the restaurant. She got a table for

two by the window and watched out for his arrival. She heard him before she saw him—the distinctive growl of the Harley's engine.

He rolled the back wheel to the curb and lifted the helmet from his head. Sliding from the bike, he tucked the helmet beneath one arm and strode into the restaurant.

Worn denim encased his long legs and his boots clumped across the wood floor of the restaurant. He pulled out the chair across from her. "Waiting long?"

Actually, she'd just arrived, but he didn't need to know she'd made a stop. "Not too long. You changed."

"I couldn't keep running around in a suit all day."

"I hear you." She tugged at the lapels of her jacket. "Did you get everything you need for my place?"

"I packed a bag. I'll pick it up after lunch." He tapped the table. "The service isn't usually this slow here. You don't even have a drink."

"I, uh, waited."

Two minutes later Judd had an iced tea in front of him and she had a sparkling water. Fortunately the waitstaff hadn't recognized her, or if they had, they didn't let on.

"Nothing from the police yet about Griff or my phone?"

He crunched a piece of ice and held up his finger. "Got a call from Detective Curtis. As we figured, the texts sent to your phone came from a disposable phone that can't even be pinged. It must've been destroyed already."

"Great." She squeezed the slice of lemon into her water. "I suppose I can understand why the burglars murdered Griff. He saw them and they wanted to keep him quiet. But why involve me? Even if I hadn't discovered the body, I would've found out about the murder."

"Scare tactic."

"But why? They already broke into my place. All this would make more sense if they sent me some kind of message. Are they trying to scare me into doing something or not doing something? How can I comply when I don't know what they want?"

"You're attributing way too much logic to a couple of thieves and murderers. Maybe one's a psychopath and likes playing mind games."

She slumped in her seat. "That makes me feel a lot better."

His hand shot out and covered hers for a brief moment. "I'm sorry. You didn't strike me as the type of client who wants me to hide things. You asked how Griff died yesterday, and I told you because you deserve the truth. But maybe you don't want that truth."

"Just give it to me." She sucked the lemon juice from her fingers and her mouth puckered.

Judd's blue eyes deepened in color and intensity. She had not calculated her actions to get a response from him, but it seemed to happen naturally.

If they'd met in a bar or at a party, they'd be in bed by now. Or maybe the old London would've headed down that path. The CEO London would shake his hand and leave him her card.

"I promise to always tell you the truth." He held up two fingers like a Boy Scout.

He'd tell her the truth but deny the attraction that sizzled between them.

It gave her an excuse to keep her secrets, too.

Over lunch, they seemed to come to an unspoken agreement to keep it light. He told her funny stories about his jobs, never once revealing the names of his clients. She shared the details of her mishap in Qatar.

"The sheikh must've been furious to discover you'd taken the diamond without actually joining his harem."

She dabbed her eyes with her napkin, struggling to control her laughter. "I kept telling him it would never happen. It's not my fault he believed that diamond would seal the deal."

"I suppose it had nothing to do with the fact that you'd been admiring it, leading him to believe he'd found the key to your heart."

"It wasn't my heart he wanted to unlock." She set the napkin back in her lap.

"Didn't he have you arrested? How'd you get out of that?"

She rubbed her fingers together. "Connections and payoffs. It's the way the world works."

"I suppose you learned that at an early age."

"We all get our life lessons." She shoved her plate away from her. "What about you? What life lessons did you learn?"

"Shoot first, ask questions later."

"At five? You learned that lesson at five years old?"

He raised his eyes to the ceiling. "Maybe four."

"You're lying."

"Are you done picking at that salad?"

"Why, do you want the rest?"

"I have work to do." His tone was hard. He caught the waiter's eye. "You're not paying me to sit around eating lunch."

"But I am paying for lunch." She made a grab for the check when the waiter left it on the table, but Judd beat her to it.

"I wouldn't call this a working lunch."

"Sure it was." Her lashes fluttered despite her best efforts to keep a poker face. "What would you call?"

He pulled his wallet out of his back pocket. "We didn't discuss business."

So he wouldn't call it a date even though that was what it had felt like to her. "We got to know each other a little better, and that's business. How are you going to do your job if you don't know your client?"

"You think I knew that pop singer I worked for over in Hawaii?"

"I think this is a little different. You were protecting her from hormonal teenagers. We have no idea yet what you're protecting me from. Don't you think getting to know me better will help you figure out where the threat's coming from?"

"Are you telling me that sheikh from Qatar is out for revenge?"

"I did give the diamond back." She folded her hands on the table and pursed her lips.

"So we can cross him off the list."

"Anyone else you've crossed off the list?"

"Nope. I'm glad I got to meet a lot of the players at your office today—your cousin, your half brother, your fiancé, your fiancé's father."

"Roger is *not* my fiancé." She flicked her fingers against his forearm.

"Will I get a chance to see them again? Most of them viewed me as the hired help, which works."

"There's something coming up this weekend, a social event."

"Argh." He sank his head in his hands and grasped his hair. "Another suit? I've worn more suits and tuxes this week than I have all year."

"What are you worried about? You certainly do them justice." Her gaze meandered across his wide shoulders. He looked better in a tux than any man she'd ever seen. It had to be because it looked as if he could burst out of it at any moment.

"They're uncomfortable." He ran his finger along the neckline of his T-shirt as if just thinking about a shirt and tie was choking him.

"Are you going to suck it up for the sake of getting close to my adversaries?"

"I will suck it up." He pushed back from the table and picked up his helmet. "But right now I'm going to scan your place for bugs."

"Can I borrow your phone?"

"What for?" He dragged it out of the pocket of his jacket.

"I need to call another taxi."

"Hop on the back of my bike."

She plucked her pencil skirt away from her thigh. "In this?"

"Can't you just suck it up so I don't have to wait for you?" He pointed to her legs. "If you're that modest—and I've heard otherwise—you can always put my jacket around your waist."

"Oh, hell, why not?" She slung her briefcase across her body. "It's not as if I'm not wearing underwear."

"I think you'll discover most CEOs do, but then, what do I know?"

Once outside, Judd grabbed the handlebars of his bike and flipped up the kickstand as she fished her sunglasses out of her purse.

"What's this?" Judd swiped a piece of paper from the seat of his bike.

"A ticket?" London shoved her glasses on top of her head.

Judd hung his helmet on one handlebar and snapped the paper open with both hands. "It's a newspaper article."

"Maybe it's trash that blew onto your bike. The wind picked up this afternoon." She slipped the helmet from the bike and fiddled with the strap.

"London."

Judd's tone of voice stilled her fingers. "What is it?"

"It's an old newspaper article about the SFPD police commission—and your father."

Chapter Nine

London's stomach dipped as her gaze scanned the sidewalk for the messenger. Were they being followed? "You're kidding."

He waved the neatly clipped article in her face. "No."

"Does it have a date?" She held out her hand, wiggling her fingers.

He handed the article to her. "No date, but it names your father on the commission, so what year was that?"

She scanned the words of the article. "Theodore didn't say, did he? But he mentioned it was at the time of the Phone Book Killer. Wait, the article even mentions the Phone Book Killer."

"Who put this on my bike and why?"

Her father's laptop burned a hole in her briefcase. She shouldn't have any secrets from him. Well, almost none.

"I think we need to get to the bottom of this, Judd. It all means something. No way would my father leave me a note about your father if it weren't important, if he didn't know something or wasn't involved in some way. My father wouldn't randomly feel sorry for your family. I wouldn't call him a cold man, but he wasn't overly sentimental, either."

"I guess we can do some research on the commission at that time, but I don't see how that's helping you with your safety, especially if someone is following you."

She shrugged. "Let's change the contract. You're a P.I. in addition to a bodyguard. I'm making an amendment to our arrangements. I want you to help me with this mystery, the purpose behind my father's note. I'll up your retainer."

"No need. You're paying me plenty to cover a few searches on the internet."

"We can do more than that." She patted her briefcase. "I have something to show you when we get back to my place."

"Related to that newspaper article?"

"Related to all of it."

"Then let's get going. I need to pick up my equipment at the office first."

He straddled his Harley as she creased the article and dropped it into her purse.

He tilted the bike to the side and she hiked up her skirt almost to her hips and climbed on. Once seated, she wrapped the arms of his jacket around her waist, draping the soft leather over her thighs.

He revved the engine, and they zoomed away from the curb. After darting in and out of traffic, he rolled to a stop in front of the building that housed his professional digs.

While he jogged up to his office, she stayed seated on the bike, not wanting to rearrange her skirt again.

He returned with a black bag and tapped her leg. "I need to put this in the saddlebag."

She shifted and curled back her leg as Judd opened the saddlebag and stuffed the black bag inside. His hand brushed her bare calf, and then he cinched her ankle and placed her foot back on the footrest.

"Don't want you falling off."

This time London held on to Judd for dear life—not because he took the turns any faster than last time or sped up and down the hills any faster, but because she didn't want to pretend anymore that this attraction didn't exist between them.

In Judd, she'd found a kindred free spirit. He didn't pass judgment on her past actions. He was down-to-earth and had no pretensions and treated her like a normal person.

That lunch had felt too much like a date, and she felt too connected to him now to return to some kind of professional relationship, which they'd never really had to begin with.

So she snuggled against his back, as close as the helmet would allow, and gripped his hips with her knees.

Judd pulled up to her building. With the motorcycle idling at the curb, London scrambled off, tugging at her skirt beneath the leather jacket around her waist. She pulled off the helmet and handed it to Judd when he climbed off the bike.

A new security guard greeted them in the lobby, and London crossed the marble floor to introduce herself. "I'm London Breck. You're the new guy?"

He stood up, holding himself as stiffly as a military man. "Yes, ma'am. I'm Paul Madden."

"Nice to meet you, Paul. This is Judd Brody. He's my... bodyguard."

If Paul found it odd she had a bodyguard, he didn't let it show on his stern face. He shook Judd's hand. "Sir, if you need anything from me, I'm at your disposal."

When they got to the elevator, Judd dipped his head and whispered in her ear, "He's a far cry from Griff."

"Too bad management didn't have him in place yesterday. Those thugs never would've gotten into my home."

Judd tensed beside her when she unlocked her door, but this time not a magazine was out of place.

As soon as the door shut, he dug into his bag and said, "I'm going to do a quick sweep of this room before we check out the computer, and then you can show me what you got."

While Judd scanned the great room, she dropped her briefcase and got some water. Watching him do his thing, she pulled the laptop from the case and settled it on the coffee table.

When he was done, he stuffed his instruments back into his bag and sat next to her. "Are you ready?"

She flipped open the computer and said, "It's in here. It's my father's laptop."

"You took it from the office?"

"Yes." He didn't have to know where, exactly.

"I'm confused. Haven't you already been working on your father's computer? How could you take over his duties without all his files and data at your fingertips?"

"Not—" she tapped the keyboard to wake it up and entered the password "—this one."

"Is that his personal computer?" In two long steps, he was at her side.

"It's personal and business. He used it to back up important files from his work computer, but I know he kept other information on it."

"Who else had access to it since his death?" He leaned over her shoulder, his hair tickling her cheek.

He had one lock of hair that always curled into his eye, and her fingers tingled with the thought of brushing it back from his forehead.

She clicked a few more keys, launching some folders. "Nobody. My father locked up this laptop. I'm not sure anyone knew of its existence except me, and maybe Mary. But even Mary didn't know where he hid it."

"Okay. Let's get searching." He patted the cushion of the couch and she sat down. He sat next to her and she dipped toward him, her shoulder brushing his.

Her bare thigh pressed against the rough denim of his

jeans, but this time he didn't move away from her. Progress. Maybe the lunch had changed the direction of his feelings, too.

She blew out a breath. "As you may know, my father and I weren't that close."

He leaned back against the couch and rested one booted foot on his knee. "From all the news stories about you over the years, I figured you were Daddy's little princess."

"Why would you think that?"

"I don't know. You pretty much did as you pleased, and he'd always rescue you. Didn't it work like that?"

"I suppose so, but he didn't consider me his princess— more like a thorn in his side. I often think he left me in charge of the company to get back at me for all those years of hell I put him through."

"And if he did?"

"I deserve it. I did put him through hell."

"You were a little girl without a mom."

Her nose tingled and the memory of rose-scented hugs feathered across her senses. She stretched her lips into a smile. "I don't know if I can blame all my craziness on being motherless."

"Sure you can." He traced the line of her jaw with the rough pad of his finger.

"Do you?"

His finger froze at the end of her chin and he sucked in a breath. "I had a mother."

"Yes, yes, your mother, but you missed your father." She dabbled her fingers down his forearm. "Is that what made you the tatted-up, Harley-riding badass?"

His chest rose and fell with a deep breath, and London held hers, wondering if she'd gone too far with him.

His thick, dark lashes fell halfway over his eyes and his mouth lifted at one corner. "Naw, I'm just naturally a badass."

She punched him in the arm to break the tension that had built up between them. She'd rather plant a kiss on his sexy mouth, but she knew Judd Brody wanted to be the hunter and not the prey.

He rose to his feet, stomping his boots. "I will leave you to deciphering your father's secret computer while I continue searching the rest of your place." She let him go, watching him from the corner of her eye as he pawed through his bag, pulling out unidentifiable bits and pieces.

"I'll start upstairs and work my way down."

She waved her hand. "Be my guest."

He pointed to his motorcycle boots. "Should I take these off? I should've asked you that before."

"I'm not that picky. Take them off if you want to."

"Since I may need to climb on top of some chairs, maybe I should." He pulled off his boots and lined them up at the fireplace.

The masculine shoes looked incongruous in her decidedly feminine place, but she liked them there.

After she watched him disappear up the stairs, she turned her attention back to her father's computer. She tried searching for the words *police, commission, Brody, Phone Book.* Nothing.

She reread the article that had been left on Judd's bike. It discussed her father's appointment to the police commission. Richard Taylor had also been on the commission at that time. Had he left the article for Judd? Why?

Had it come from Mary? Somehow she couldn't picture her father's secretary skulking around the streets of North Beach looking for Judd's motorcycle.

Who had left it for him and why? Or maybe it was intended for her? If someone knew she had Judd on her payroll, maybe he figured Judd would turn the article over to her.

It could be same person who'd texted her. She let the article drift to the coffee table. How had that thought crept into her head? Her father's note about Joseph Brody's innocence had nothing to do with the current threats against her. In fact, she'd been using Spencer's note to escape the realities of the break-in, Theodore's beating and Griff's murder.

She typed in another search, and while scanning the results, realized she'd been searching for files only. She entered *police* again and expanded the search to all items.

She blinked when several picture files appeared in the list. He'd kept pictures on this laptop?

She clicked through the pictures and discovered several of her father with the commission. He must've scanned those onto this computer.

She dragged them all into another folder and printed them out. Then she clicked on the pictures icon.

She gasped and the hand hovering over the directional mouse trembled when she saw the picture folder called "Madeline."

He couldn't. He didn't.

Lodging her tongue in the corner of her mouth, she double clicked on the folder. Neat yellow folders organized by date populated the monitor. She clicked on the first chronological folder.

Her eyes flooded with tears and she covered her mouth with one hand as her gaze locked on the blond-haired tot in the sandbox. Her heart thumped painfully in her chest as she launched each picture in succession. Each image sucked more air out of her lungs until she felt suffocated.

Where had he gotten these? Why?

A heavy step on the stair had her snapping the laptop closed on the bright-eyed girl with the happy grin.

She pressed the heels of her hands to her eyes and then wiped her hand across her nose. She coughed. "All clear?"

"Haven't found anything yet. Have you?"

Oh, yeah. She'd found more than she'd bargained for.

"Some pictures." She opened the laptop and closed the Madeline folder. "One of my father and the rest of the police commission the year he was appointed."

"Well, that's something. He must've taken the trouble to scan those in, since I don't think digital cameras were all that common twenty years ago."

He aimed some device at the wall and moved it across the area.

"I was thinking the same thing. It must mean something for him to have taken that trouble."

Judd held something that looked like a microphone up to the four corners of the room.

London ran her hands over her warm face and scooped her hair into a ponytail. "Is that thing supposed to beep or something if it finds anything?"

"Sort of. I can't detect any evidence of bugs in your place. It's lookin' good."

"That's a relief. Maybe it's over, Judd."

"What do you mean?"

"Someone tried to ruffle my feathers, but it's not working. Maybe they're done now. I attended the board meeting today as CEO."

"I'd feel better about that theory if Griff's body hadn't been hanging outside the trash room of your building. That's more than ruffled feathers, wouldn't you say?"

"Of course. I didn't mean to make light of Griff's death at all. Maybe that part of it was a big mistake."

"And the text messages leading you to his body? Those were a mistake, too? Somebody wants to do more than ruffle your feathers, London."

She jumped up, tossing her hair over one shoulder. "If someone wants to kill me, why doesn't he just take his best shot?"

"Hey." He dropped his microphone and took her by the

shoulders. "Don't say that. Nobody's going to hurt you. Not while I'm on the job."

She didn't break away from him and he didn't let go. Instead she stared into those fierce blue eyes—ferocity on her behalf.

"Judd, do you think it's all connected?"

"What?"

"The threats, the note, the article, your father, my father—us."

His grip on her shoulders softened into a caress. "How?"

"I'm not sure. It occurred to me when I was looking through the pictures on my father's laptop. Why now? Why did Mary deliver the note? Who put the article on your bike? Someone's tracking our movements—yours and mine."

"Maybe it's all one big coincidence, London."

She ran her thumb between his eyebrows, smoothing out the crease there. "You don't really believe that. Stop trying to make me feel better. We both know none of this is coincidence. How did you wind up taking that job for Bunny anyway?"

"I told you. A buddy of mine had the job and couldn't make it."

"Why not?"

"I don't know. I didn't ask. He called, said he had an easy gig with good pay and needed someone to cover for him."

"Had you ever covered for him before?"

"No, he always needs the money." His hands slid from her shoulders to her upper arms. "I'm glad I did cover for him."

"I am, too. It's almost like fate. Our pasts are tied together somehow."

He traced his finger along her jaw. "It's not just the past, is it?"

Her lips parted as she panted out a breath. Would he acknowledge the connection they had in the present? Should she? She needed to tread lightly. You didn't corner a man like Judd Brody.

"Whatever is in our pasts is affecting the present. Forces beyond our control are bringing us together, and those same forces are going to bring us resolution."

Judd threw back his head and laughed. Then he tapped her temple lightly. "I think you're getting carried away with all the fate stuff."

His laugh had broken the spell and brought her back to earth. "You're right. It's looking into the past, plus the time of day."

He glanced out the large window with the view of the city, lights twinkling in the office buildings. "The sun's going down and I'm just about finished."

He turned abruptly from the window and stopped. He swayed to one side and then the other.

"What's wrong?"

"A light. I saw a glimmer of light on that wall."

"That's wallpaper."

"I know." He crept across the room on silent feet. Extending his arms, he ran his hands across a portion of the wall. "London."

"What are you doing?" His manner and his voice had her heart tripping over itself in her chest.

He pressed his fingers against a spot on the wall. "Turn on the lights."

She stumbled toward the lamp next to the couch and turned the switch. "What do you see? Is it a bug? I thought your secret-agent equipment didn't detect any of those."

"It's not—" he scratched his fingernails against the wallpaper "—a bug."

"I don't get it." She swallowed, her throat dry.

He landed his fist against the wall. "What's on the other side of this wall?"

"It's the other unit, the one I bought to have the floor to myself." She inched toward him and the…thing on her wall.

"What's in that other unit?"

"Nothing. It's empty. Are you going to tell me what's going on? What did you find?"

He stepped back and tapped the wallpaper. "Look."

Licking her lips, she leaned forward. A round piece of glass or clear plastic caught the light. "What is that?"

"It's a simple device that's allowing someone to see into your place."

"Th-that's crazy. There's nothing next door. There's nobody there."

"Do you have the key? We're going over there right now."

She headed for the kitchen, glancing over her shoulder at the wall. Judd had this all wrong. The walls in this building were too thick to allow something like that.

She opened a cabinet and lifted a key ring from the rack. She twirled it around her finger. "This is it."

He followed her into the hallway, and she jerked her thumb to the left. "The front door's that way."

When Judd reached for the weapon he'd shoved in his waistband, her heart started to gallop. She turned the key in the lock and Judd stepped forward, tucking her behind him.

It reminded her of the other night. What would they find this time?

He pushed the door open and walked into the entryway, leading with his gun.

The layout of the condo mimicked her own, and she followed Judd down the two steps into the unfurnished great room. She flicked on the switch to the chandelier that hung above the dining area, and her nostrils twitched as an unpleasant smell wafted toward them. "What is that smell?"

Judd lifted his nose to the air. "Smells like garbage…or something rotting."

"M-maybe a rat got in here and died."

"While eating take-out pizza?" He pointed to the large kitchen island that separated the kitchen from the dining area, littered with two pizza boxes.

"What the hell?" She stomped toward the boxes and flipped up a cardboard lid. Half-eaten pieces of pizza emitted a rank odor and she pinched her nose as she gagged.

"Looks as though someone has been making himself at home. Where's the common wall with your living room?"

"It's back this way. It's a downstairs office or bedroom. The whole place is unfurnished. With my father's death and taking over the company, I haven't had time to remodel yet."

She led the way and he followed close on her heels. She pushed open the door and pressed the light switch on the wall.

A bubble of fear rose in her throat as her gaze tripped over a pillow on the floor next to the wall.

"I—I didn't put that there."

Still gripping his gun, Judd squeezed past her into the room and headed for the pillow. "Your living room is on the other side of this wall." He pressed his hand against the wall's surface and a piece shifted and fell to the floor.

London jumped back. "What is that?"

"Someone sawed out a piece of the wall." He kicked it with his toe, then crouched down and stuck his head in the hollow of the wall. Then he cursed, his voice muffled. "London, you have to see this."

She willed her feet to move across the floor even though they felt like lead blocks. She knelt beside him, taking little comfort in his solid shoulder pressing against hers.

"Put your eye to that plastic circle embedded in the drywall."

He shifted to the side and she ducked her head, pressing her eye against the circle. She yelped at the panoramic view of her great room. "That's my place."

"Someone has been watching you, London. Watching you from this room."

Chapter Ten

London fell backward and he caught her in his arms, holding her against his chest.

Trembles passed through her body like waves and he rested his cheek against her hair. "Are you okay?"

She turned her head to look into his face, her eyes huge and round. "I can't believe someone would do something like this. How in the hell did he even get in here?"

"It doesn't look like anyone's been here for a few days. Maybe he was worried that he'd be discovered after Griff's murder and left." He wrapped an arm around her waist and pulled her away from the wall. They both landed on the floor with her halfway in his lap.

She folded one leg beneath her and leaned against his thigh. "Do you think Griff let them up here? I can imagine they gave him some line about getting some stories on the people who live in this building. Griff told us he'd cooperated with the paparazzi before."

She seemed to have recovered some of her composure—but she stayed in his lap.

"That could be. He mentioned that he'd done it before without any bad consequences. I don't see how a stranger or maybe more than one stranger could make his way into this unit, cut a chunk out of the wall, order pizza and spy on you without someone in this building helping him out."

She gathered his T-shirt in her fists. "Maybe if we leave everything as is and pretend we never found his little squirrel hole, he'll come back and we can catch *him* in the act."

"I think the game is up for him. He literally destroyed his contact in this building by killing Griff. He's not going to try to buy off another security guard—especially that guy down there now."

She released his shirt and rubbed her eyes, her knuckles digging into her sockets. "Now I'm sitting here thinking about all the stuff I did in that room over the past few weeks. Who knows? Maybe even longer than that."

"None of that dancing naked on the tabletops?" He tugged the end of one blond lock of hair hanging over her shoulder.

She rewarded him with a shaky smile. "I thought I told you, all that stuff is behind me."

"Why?" He clinched the strand of hair and wound it around his finger. "Why are you trying so hard to run away from the old London? She sounds like a lot of fun."

"The old London made a lot mistakes."

"How many mistakes can a twentysomething make?"

Her green eyes clouded over, and she stared out the window over his shoulder. "You'd be surprised."

"Do you think London Breck the CEO isn't going to make mistakes? All you can do is be true to yourself."

"Do you follow your own advice, Judd Brody?"

"I try." He held her gaze even though the lie burned in his gut.

"Right." She fell back on the floor, crossing her arms behind her head and staring at the ceiling. "I have a new wrinkle to our contract."

"Oh?" He stretched out beside her, digging his elbow into the carpet and propping up his head. Was she going to put a moratorium on personal conversations?

She rolled her head to the side. "I want you to move in—here."

He blinked. Move in to a posh Nob Hill condo? Next door to London Breck? He could do that.

"Do you want me to watch you through that peephole?"

She flung her arm out to the side, smacking him in the belly. "No. If you don't mind roughing it, we can set up something for you to sleep on. I'd just feel safer having you close by."

"I'm not going anywhere." He took her hand, threaded his fingers through hers and pulled it back onto his stomach. "I'm going to figure out who's threatening you and why, and then I'm going to put a stop to it."

She squeezed his hand. "Judd, I think it has something to do with my father's death, and I think it has something to do with the note he left me, which means it has something to do with your father."

"I think you're right."

"Aren't you curious about why your father jumped from the bridge? Especially now that his name has been cleared of the Phone Book slayings?"

That familiar tightness crept into his neck and jaw. "He probably thought he was being set up and didn't see a way out. Or he'd already planned to kill himself and the situation offered the perfect excuse. Either way, he took the coward's way out."

She sat up, dragging her hand away from his. "You're right. It does seem as if he *was* set up to take the fall. Certain items were found in his personal belongings, items that didn't belong to him, right?"

His heart tapped out a staccato beat. "Yes."

"Someone must've put them there, planted them so that suspicion would fall on him."

"My brother Ryan figured it was the real Phone Book Killer, Russ Langford. The man was a psychopath who murdered his wife and then went on a killing spree to cover the deed. Ryan believed Langford set up my father, too."

"Did he admit to it?"

"No. He was killed by a police sniper before he did too much talking to Ryan."

"Did Ryan investigate any further?"

"It was a touchy situation. It turned out the writer who'd been helping him, Kacie Manning, was Russ Langford's daughter. She'd believed my father had killed her mother and then discovered it was her own father."

Her jaw dropped and she pressed her fingers against her lips. "And Ryan didn't want to look into it any further?"

"By the time they'd made the discovery, Ryan had fallen in love with Kacie. He took her back to Crestview with him, and his primary focus now is protecting Kacie and helping her heal from the revelations."

"That's sweet and all, but this is your father."

He didn't need London telling him that. "I think it's safe to say that Langford set him up."

She raised her brows. "If you were working that case for me, I'd fire you. Shouldn't a P.I. be curious about everything? You're leaving no stone unturned for me. Why not do the same for yourself?"

He rubbed a hand across his mouth. "It's different, London. Nobody's threatening me. My father's already been vindicated."

"Not really."

"Sure he has. Langford admitted to being the Phone Book Killer, the newspaper printed a big article, case closed."

"Except your father jumped from the Golden Gate Bridge for some inexplicable reason."

He opened his mouth, but she held up her hand. "And you can't forgive him for that."

His back stiffened, his repose no longer comfortable or relaxing. "I guess that's something for me to deal with."

He rolled to his stomach and army crawled back to the wall. Then he sat up, picking up the piece of drywall and fitting it back into place. "As soon as I bring the rest of my stuff here, I'm going to dig that spy device out of the wall and patch this up."

"Should we try to get fingerprints?"

"You can call the cops and tell them you had a squatter here. They'll dust the place, but I doubt you'll find anything. Someone is not going to go through all this trouble and then leave a set of prints."

"It's getting late." She rubbed her belly. "And I'm hungry despite the disgusting smell in the other room."

"If you want to change, I'll take you out to get something to eat and we can drop by my place to pick up my stuff." He tapped the wall. "Do you even have a car here in the city?"

"I do. It's in the garage downstairs, but I don't drive it much when I'm here. Since Dad's death, Theodore's been insisting on driving me around in that limo. But he keeps that at Dad's place in Pacific Heights. Besides—" she leaped to her feet like a ballerina "—I like riding on the back of that Harley."

And he liked her there, her arms wrapped around him, her body pressed against his. He could get used to that.

"Okay, let's lock up and get some food."

She tugged at her skirt. "I'll change first."

"I'll come with you, but let me get rid of some of this trash first."

After this discovery, he didn't want to leave London alone for a second. Maybe she had a stalker. Maybe it had nothing to do with her father—or his.

He studied her profile as she locked up the condo, her jaw still hard and her mouth still tight. The stress had her all wound up. She didn't need to hear his new theory right now.

She waited for him by her own door while he dumped the pizza boxes into the trash chute. When he joined her, she dangled the key out to him. "You can take this one. I'm going to slip into some motorcycle-riding clothes."

"I guess that means someplace casual for dinner."

"I attend enough galas and functions and benefits where I have to get all decked out. Casual is good."

While she changed, he wandered to the big window that took up the majority of her east-facing wall. She had a view that commanded the best of the city—this city full of secrets and lies. Since he'd opened up shop as a P.I., it seemed as if he'd been privy to half of those secrets and lies.

But he'd never taken a shot at why his old man had killed himself. Didn't want to. Had never wanted to dig that deeply. Never wanted to care that much.

He had to admit that he'd allowed events outside of his control to dictate his life, just as much as London had. Why did she want this CEO gig so badly when she hated it and was ill suited for it?

London jogged downstairs, a pair of black jeans stuffed into some boots and a powder-blue sweater that looked as soft as a cloud hugging her body. She made casual look decidedly upscale…and hot.

Judd tapped on the window. "That's the Bohemian Club."

She sidled next to him and leaned her forehead against the window. "Yeah, it's the old Fleck Mansion. Now that creepy men's club has it. My father was a member."

He mulled over the implication of her words, but before he had a chance to respond, she spun away from the window and called over her shoulder, "This time I'll wear my own motorcycle jacket."

"Is that the one you wore over that fancy dress the other night?"

"Yep." She pulled it from the closet in the foyer.

"Trying to make a statement?"

"I know I should've worn some tasteful stole or even, God forbid, a mink with that dress."

He opened the front door for her and narrowed his eyes. "You own mink?"

"No, I do not. Why? Would you throw red paint on me if I did?"

"I, uh—" he cleared his throat "—sort of have a thing for animals."

"Do you have any?"

"A fish tank."

She tilted her head as she took the helmet from his hands. "That's quite a commitment."

"I like animals. My brother Sean got me a mixed-breed mutt when I was a kid, and that dog, Prince, was my best friend." He secured the helmet on her head and buckled the chin strap, resisting the urge to flip up the visor and kiss her.

How did she manage to get this stuff out of him? He hadn't told anyone about Prince in years. When that dog died the year before he enlisted in the marines, it broke his heart. He didn't need to go that far and tell her *that*.

She tipped up the visor. "What happened to Prince?"

"Died of old age."

She studied his face for a few moments and then tipped the visor back down. "Where are we eating?"

"Do you like Indian food?"

"Sure. I know a place—"

He cut her off. "I know a place. It's on the edge of the Tenderloin, close to Union Square, so it's not too dicey."

He straddled the bike and tilted it to the side so she could climb on the back. "Hang on."

She obliged him, and his blood simmered as she tightened her arms around his waist. He could ride forever with London hanging on to him. He could use a long ride up the coast right now—take her away from all this, away from BGE, set her free.

Instead he wove through the city streets, stopping at signals as the transients shuffled in the crosswalks and the lights of the shops twinkled in Union Square beyond.

He pulled up to the curb in front of the restaurant. He shook his finger in her face as he loosened the strap on the helmet. "Don't get any ideas about slumming it in any bars down here."

"Don't worry." She pointed to the sidewalk. "This street is okay, but the one back there is sketchy."

"Funny how the good, the bad and the ugly exist side by side in this city, isn't it?"

"That's part of its charm."

"Would you live anywhere else?"

"No, would you?"

"Don't think so."

They stepped into the restaurant and the smells of curry and meats sizzling from the tandoori oven blasted him.

Judd requested and got a table by the window so he could watch his bike. He didn't want any more surprises—no newspaper articles pinned to his seat.

London stuck to the vegetarian dishes, and he stuck to drinking water.

He tapped her empty wineglass. "Feel free to have a drink. I never have even one while I'm riding my bike, but I don't mind if you do."

"I'm good. I hate drinking alone."

He tore off a piece of naan and dipped the bread in a green chutney. "Tell me about this fund-raiser you're dragging me to."

She huffed out a breath. "I'm not dragging you there. You want to see some of the players in action, right?"

"Sure I do. Where is it?"

"It's at the War Memorial Opera House."

He stopped chewing and took a gulp of water. "It's not the ballet. Tell me it's not the ballet."

"It's not the ballet…exactly."

"What does that mean?"

"My father was a big supporter of the arts in the city, and this is his annual fund-raiser for the ballet and the symphony. There are a few members of the ballet troupe who attend, and they usually perform—not a full-scale ballet or anything." She smirked. "Not a big fan of the ballet, I take it?"

"You could say that."

"It should be painless."

"Tux required?"

"Naturally."

He shook his head. "Never had to wear a tux for the pop princess."

They spent dinner covering dangerous ground again—sharing stories, feelings and more than a few laughs. He kept telling himself that London needed this break, that keeping her stress level down made his job easier.

That was what he told himself.

They finished dinner and on the sidewalk Judd handed London the helmet and grabbed his handlebars.

His phone buzzed in his pocket, and he leaned the bike back on its kickstand. "I have a call coming in."

London clamped the helmet between her arm and body. "Take it."

He pulled the phone out of his pocket and glanced at the display. "Unknown number. Hello?"

"Is this Judd Brody?"

"Yeah. Who's this?"

"Not important."

"I'd say it is, since you called me."

London tapped him on the arm, and he looked at her and shrugged.

"I have some information. Are you interested or not?"

"What kind of information?"

London kept tugging on his sleeve and he held a finger to his lips even though she hadn't said a word. Then he punched the speaker button for her.

"I'm not gonna say too much over the phone. I have the goods on how it all started."

London folded her arms around the helmet and hugged it to her chest while mouthing words he couldn't understand.

"How what all started? If this is legit, just tell me."

"Oh, it's legit, but I'm not staying on this phone long enough to give you the whole story. I'll meet you after that party tomorrow night, in the alley behind the symphony hall at midnight."

London sucked in a quick breath.

"How do you know about that?" Judd gripped the phone, his knuckles turning white.

"Stop asking so many questions and just be there...be there if you wanna find out what happened to Joey Brody."

Chapter Eleven

The line went dead and Judd stood on the curb staring at the phone.

London snatched it out of his hand and hit the redial button. The phone rang, but nobody picked it up.

He'd recovered from his stupor and shook his head back and forth, his shaggy hair brushing the collar of his leather jacket. "What the hell is going on?"

She pushed Redial again, her heart beating double-time. "It sounds to me as if the pieces are coming together."

"If someone wants to start passing on info about my father, that person would be better off giving it to my brother Sean. He's the cop. He spent most of his adult life trying to figure out what happened."

She disconnected the call again. "Sean's not working with me."

"What does that mean?" He grabbed the handlebars of his bike and kicked up the stand.

"My mystery, your mystery—they're linked. You have to see that now, Judd. Someone left that newspaper clipping about my father on your bike, not mine." She stuffed the helmet on her head and grabbed the straps with both hands. "Why now? Why you? I'll answer your questions. Now because your father has been cleared of the suspicions around him, and you because you're helping me."

"Hop on, and redial that number once more before I start the engine. We can try it again at the next light." He shoved the keys in the bike's ignition.

She punched the button again and the phone rang three times. Then a woman answered it.

"Who's this keeps calling? Jonny, baby. Is that you?"

London asked, "Who's this?"

"You called this phone. I ain't sayin' squat."

"Wait, wait. Someone called me from this phone. I'm just trying to figure out who it was. Is this your phone?"

"This is a pay phone, bitch, on one of my corners. You tryin' to shake your moneymaker in my territory?"

London choked. "Absolutely not, girlfriend. Some skank called my man from this phone, and I wanna know who it is."

The woman laughed. "Bitch, this is a working girls' corner, so if someone's calling your man from this phone, he's gettin' a little something-something on the side."

London screamed, "Where is it? Where is this corner?"

"It's at Sixteenth and Folsom in the Mission District, baby. And you can tell that skank Daisy sent you."

"Thanks, Daisy." London ended the call. "Did you hear all that?"

Judd twisted around in his seat with raised eyebrows and an open mouth. "Maybe you *would* make a good CEO after all."

Daisy's corner was a few miles south of them, and after convincing Judd he didn't need to take her home first, they rolled down Folsom Street, crossing underneath the freeway. The Mission didn't lack for nightlife, and a mixture of transients, hookers, partiers and clueless tourists milled around the streets.

When they idled at a red light, she tapped on Judd's shoulder and yelled in his ear, "It must be in that gas station."

He nodded once and when the light changed, he veered into the right lane and turned into the station.

A few ladies of the night gave Judd the once-over, watching him dismount from the bike. When London slid from the seat, took off the helmet and shook out her hair, the streetwalkers dispersed, on the prowl for likelier johns.

Judd ambled toward the phone booth, its glass scarred and cracked. "This must be it."

She held up her finger. "Hang on. I'm going to do a re-dial of the number to make sure."

He rested his hand on the receiver while she pressed the redial button on his cell phone. The shrill ring from the phone booth startled her, even though she was expecting it.

Judd picked up the receiver and spoke into the mouth-piece. "I'm amazed this thing still works."

"Well, it does, and this is the phone he used to call you. Turns out Daisy's no liar."

Replacing the phone in its cradle, Judd turned outward, facing the rest of the gas station and the street. "We verified the phone, but the caller didn't hang around to see if I could trace it."

"We could ask in there." She jerked her thumb over her shoulder at the cashier's window.

"The clerk's sitting behind bulletproof glass. I doubt he's going to give us anything."

"You're a P.I. You haven't greased a few palms in your day?"

He rolled his eyes. "If I did, I'm sure I didn't call it *greasing palms*."

"Oh, do they only say that in the movies?"

"Pretty much."

Judd hunched toward the window and rapped on the glass with one knuckle.

The clerk turned away from the TV he'd been glued to

and drew his bushy brows over his nose. "What do you want? I know you're not buying gas."

"I could." Judd tipped his chin toward the pay phone. "Who have you seen use that phone in the past half hour?"

"Nobody." The cashier turned back to the fight on TV.

Before London could reach for her purse, Judd dragged a bill from the front pocket of his jeans, wadded it up and rolled it into the tray beneath the window. "Past half hour? The man before the hooker answered the phone."

"There's no hooking around here." The cashier snatched up the bill.

"Of course not." Judd dug into his pocket again. "The man before that sweet girl was on the phone with her pastor?"

This time the man turned to face them. When he reached for the second bill in the cash tray, Judd plucked it away.

The cashier scratched his black stubble. "I might've seen a guy on the phone earlier. White guy, baseball cap. He might've even come up here to buy some smokes."

Judd dipped into his pocket again, and crumpled the money in his fist, which he rested on the metal ledge of the cashier's window. "Smoker, huh?"

"Ten gallons on number two!" a man yelled from the pumps.

The cashier flipped a couple of switches and returned his focus to Judd's face. "He was a hard-looking dude, prison tats on his neck, nose broken a few times. I'd guess ex-con. Middle-aged, around forty. Can't tell you much else. He was wearing sunglasses—at night—and he had that cap low on his face. Clean shaven. And I never told you nothin'."

"Nothing at all." Judd flicked the rolled-up bill into the tray and slipped a twenty in after. "And give me twenty bucks on number four."

London grabbed his arm as he strode back to his bike. "Ex-con. Do you believe him?"

"I believe the cashier thinks the man was an ex-con. Whether he was or not is another issue."

"But we're meeting him tomorrow, right?"

"We?"

"It's my function, it's my case and you're working for me."

"Ouch." He picked up the nozzle, squeezed a few times and replaced it in the pump. "I was wondering when you were going to play that card."

"What card?" She folded her arms, knowing damn well what card. "There is no card. I want in on this information. It's all part of the same investigation."

He climbed on the bike and tilted it for her to straddle the back. "You're getting kind of carried away with this P.I. stuff, aren't you? You're supposed to be a CEO. CEOs don't zoom around on Harleys meeting ex-cons."

Wrapping her arms around his waist, she slipped her hands beneath his T-shirt and dug her nails into his flat belly. "Now who's playing a card?"

"What card?" He tensed the muscles in his stomach so that it felt as though her nails were scraping granite.

"The CEO card. Do you think you can stop me from doing something by pointing out it's not something a CEO would do?"

He laughed and started his engine. "Thought it was worth a try."

"You know, I can always hire another P.I.—one who appreciates my efforts."

"No other P.I. can give you what I can give you. Now, can you get your claws out of me?"

She flattened her hands and rubbed her palms against the rigid muscles of his belly. Then he took off and she flew against the backrest.

The rumble of the Harley's engine didn't allow for any more conversation, but when it became clear Judd was heading back to Nob Hill and not his place, she shouted in his ear at the next stop sign, "Are you going to get your stuff?"

"Tomorrow." He revved the engine and continued.

Did that mean he wasn't going to spend the night in the empty unit? If so, she'd have to convince him otherwise. She needed him tonight, needed him close. The two of them were on the verge of a big discovery, one that involved both of their families.

On the next downhill, she fitted her body against his, resting her helmeted head against his back. For a fleeting second, she wished all the turmoil would just go away and she could ride off with Judd into the sunset.

Her lips curved into a smile. Where would they be without the turmoil? He craved it as much as she did. Judd Brody was an adrenaline junkie through and through.

When Judd pulled up to her building, she held her breath. Would he come up?

He cut the engine and twisted around in his seat. "Where can I park this thing for the night?"

She released a long breath, fogging up the visor. She flipped it up. "Let me off and I'll enter the code for the garage. You can park it next to my car."

"Do you have an extra toothbrush?"

"Of course. You can stay on my couch again tonight until we get things set up next door."

He steadied the bike for her and she climbed off. Removing the helmet, she approached the keypad for the garage door and entered the code.

The gate slid open and Judd rolled his bike down the driveway.

She waved him toward the parking space behind hers and he wheeled the bike into place.

When he got off, he pointed to her Mini. "You're kidding me. That's what you drive?"

"You know how it is driving in this city. Isn't that why you ride a Harley?"

"One of many reasons."

He stroked the handlebars of the bike, and she shivered. Oh, to be caressed by those hands like that.

He smacked his hand against the seat and she jumped. "Are we going up or are we just going to stand around an exhaust-filled garage admiring my bike?"

When they got to her door, he held up the key to the other unit, swinging it around his finger. "I'm going to do a sweep of the place next door. Do you have a big garbage bag? I'll at least get rid of some more of that junk and that pillow."

She gave him a plastic bag. When he left, she rummaged through the cabinet in the master bath for a new toothbrush. She also folded a blanket on the edge of the couch and added the pillow he'd used the other night.

Before she dropped the pillow on the couch she buried her face in it, breathing in Judd's scent. She'd dated too many guys who went heavy on the cologne. Judd had a different essence—natural, manly. Even the smell of him made her feel safe and protected.

She unzipped her boots and pulled off her socks. She stopped short of changing into pajamas. How obvious did she want to make this seduction? Of course, there were pajamas and then there were *pajamas*. She could slip into some baggy flannels. The silk and lace would act as a sledgehammer.

The key scraped in her lock and Judd charged through her front door. He kicked it closed behind him, and before she could say one word or catch her breath, his long stride ate up the distance between them and he pulled her into his arms.

He cupped her chin with his large hand and took possession of her lips. While devouring her, he wrapped one arm around her waist and yanked her close. He fitted his pelvis against hers and she felt his erection through his jeans, her jeans and the haze of desire that had engulfed her.

He pulled away and she blinked, touching her throbbing bottom lip with her fingertips.

"What just happened?"

"Do you want this, London? Do you want me?"

If he had to ask, she hadn't been as obvious as she imagined. She couldn't even form one word. She nodded and squeaked.

"I'll take that as a yes." This time he took her face in both of his hands and got serious. He slipped his tongue into her mouth, and his kisses were as spicy as the curry they'd just consumed.

She undulated against his erection and he dropped his hands to her derriere and squeezed.

He growled. "Uh, can you hold off on that right now?"

She pressed her lips against his jaw instead and whispered, "What happened over there?"

"Over there?" He stroked one hand down her back and she felt as treasured as his Harley.

"Next door. Were you peering through the peephole and witnessed me taking off my shoes and socks and got turned on?"

His laugh turned into a growl. "I've been turned on since the minute you ripped your dress off in the alley."

Her tongue darted into his ear. "I only ripped off the bottom of my dress, and did it really take you that long?"

"Long? That was the first time I saw you."

"How soon they forget." She planted her hands against his rock-hard chest and grabbed handfuls of his T-shirt. "I've been turned on since the moment I saw you across the room at the hotel that night, and when I bumped into you."

"You bumped into me?"

"I guess I wasn't that memorable."

He snapped his fingers. "That was you. The cold blonde awash in sparkles. Untouchable."

She pulled her sweater over her head and unhooked her bra. Then she took his hands and placed them over her bare breasts. "Clearly, that's not the case."

His spiky dark lashes dropped over his eyes as he cupped her breasts and brushed his thumbs across her nipples. He hissed through his teeth. "So soft and warm for an ice princess."

She dragged her fingernails along the ink on his arm. "So sensitive and protective for a badass biker."

His eyelids flew open and he tugged at the buttons of her jeans. When they gaped open at her hips, he yanked them down to her thighs and she stepped back to peel them off.

She crossed one leg over the other, standing like a stork, and rubbed her arms. "It's chilly in here."

Before she finished the last syllable, Judd's warm, rough hands skimmed down her back and thighs. Then he cupped her bottom and hoisted her up until she wrapped her legs around his hips.

He held her against his body, strong enough for the two of them, and kissed her silly.

She tugged on his earlobe and he released her lips. "Do you want to find a bed?"

"As long as it's yours."

She untangled her legs from around his body and clutched his arm as she swayed. "You took my breath away, Judd Brody, and not for the first time."

She turned toward the stairs and extended her hand behind her. He laced his fingers with hers and she led him to the staircase.

Halfway up, he yanked her back toward him, hooked an arm around her waist and nuzzled her neck. "I could take you right here."

She turned in his arms, and being one step above him, she could stare deeply into his blue eyes. "Why now?"

"Because I like a little variety. We can do it on my Harley, too." He kissed her nose and she tugged on the lock of hair that curled beneath his ear.

"You know that's not what I mean. You've been sort of holding me at arm's length. I get that you wanted to maintain a professional relationship."

His blue eyes darkened, and she wondered if she'd ruined the moment by reminding him of his professional code.

He slipped his hands inside her panties and caressed her flesh. "It's like you said before, there's something between us, something between our stories. When this is over, we'll go our separate ways. You'll be heading your international corporation, and I'll probably be off to the Greek isles to keep an eye on some shipping magnate's daughter. Why not—" he yanked down her panties so that they puddled around her ankles "—live for the moment?"

Before she could object to the part about going their separate ways and the Greek shipping magnate's daughter, Judd caught her in his arms again and eased her back against the steps.

The Persian runner that climbed up the center of the stairs did little to cushion the hard wood beneath. Then she forgot all about the wood and the shipping magnate's daughter as Judd knelt on the stairs below her and pressed his hands on the insides of her thighs, nudging them apart.

He buried his head between her legs, and when his tongue touched her most sensitive area, she gasped and threw her head back. He probed her with his tongue, and just when she thought she couldn't stand the pleasure anymore, he burrowed inside her, bringing her to unimagined heights.

She panted his name, and he answered by planting a row

of kisses down her thigh while his finger took the place of his tongue.

She closed around him, lifting her bottom from the step.

Putting his hands beneath her, he guided her back to his mouth. He added his lips and teeth to the exquisite torture he was performing, driving her toward a precipice whose descent would surely shatter her into pieces.

He obviously didn't care. He suckled her between his lips and the world exploded behind her tightly closed eyes. She thrust her pelvis forward and then back over and over as the warm surge melted her bones.

When her climax had drained every drop of energy from her body, she collapsed on the steps like a rag doll, used and forgotten.

But Judd had no intention of forgetting her—at least not now.

He scooped her up in his arms, and her legs went around his waist again in a natural fit. As he climbed the remaining steps to the second floor, the soft cotton of his T-shirt brushed her breasts, making her nipples tingle all over again. The rough denim of his jeans chafed her sensitive flesh, still throbbing with her release.

With her curled around his body, he kicked open the door of her bedroom. "Ah, here's your bed."

He dropped her on top of the bedspread and then stood back, crossing his arms, his stance wide.

When he'd tossed her onto the bed, the lethargy from her climax had prevented her from making a move. She lay splayed across the mattress, her hair fanning out behind her, one arm dangling over the edge.

His gaze roamed over her naked body, and a slight smile hovered on his lips.

"Why—" Her voice came out as a croak, and she cleared her throat. "Why are you still completely dressed, down to your boots, and I'm stark naked?"

He cocked his head. "I thought you liked being naked. That's what all the tabloid stories say. London Breck naked in fountains. London Breck naked at the beach. London Breck naked on a yacht."

She scrambled to her knees, reached up and pressed two fingers against his soft lips, the lips that had just rocked her world. "London Breck naked and Judd Brody naked. That's all I want now."

"Come and get it." He spread his arms wide.

She pointed to his feet. "Okay, you're going to have to take off those boots yourself. I draw the line there."

He whistled. "After all that work I just did on the stairs? You *are* a diva."

She swung her legs over the side of the bed. "If you want me to…"

"Just kidding." He chucked her under the chin. He sat on the edge of the bed next to her, crossing one ankle over his knee. He pulled off one boot and then the other, peeling off his socks in the process.

She placed her hands against his back. "Stand up again. I want to do this right and I want to enjoy the view while I'm doing it."

He stood in front of her and she rolled up his T-shirt, pulling it from his massive shoulders and over his head.

Sitting back on her heels, she blew out a long breath at the sculpted figure in front of her. If she looked up the definition of *built,* a picture of Judd Brody's body would be next to it. Thick muscles bunched across his shoulders and arms, and another tattoo spilled across the chiseled muscles of his chest.

"Are you just lookin' or are you going to help me out here?"

By helping him out, she had no doubt he was referring to the bulge in his jeans.

"I'll gladly help you and help myself." She fumbled with

the button at his fly, suddenly as nervous as a virgin on her wedding night. While she tugged at the button, he plowed his fingers through her hair and whispered, "Like a silver mane, capturing all the light."

Her fingers shook as she pulled down his zipper. He had mad skills with his mouth and tongue *and* he could spout poetic lines.

She got the zipper down and peeled his pants away from the black briefs that barely contained his straining erection.

Tugging down his briefs with one hand, she caressed his smooth, tight flesh with the other. His body bucked, and she reached around and dug her fingernails into the hard muscle of his buttocks.

He sealed his mouth over hers and she deepened her strokes as he deepened the kiss.

She whispered against his mouth, "Join me on the bed."

He stepped back from her and pulled the tangle of jeans and underwear from his body. Before discarding the jeans, he reached into a pocket and pulled out two foil packs. He tossed them onto the nightstand.

She fell back against the pillows, stretching her arms over her head. "How long have you been carrying those condoms around? Or do you always keep a couple of spares in your pocket?"

He joined her on the bed, lining up his body with hers. "I've been carrying those since the moment I saved you in the alley."

She kissed her fingertips and dabbled them across his scruffy chin. "You're lying, but I don't mind a bit."

Slipping his arms on either side of her, he twirled her around so that his chest pressed against her back. He lifted her hair from the back of her neck and kissed the nape.

She wriggled against him and he prodded between her legs.

She heard the foil of the condom wrapper crackle. Then

he toyed with one breast as he smoothed his thumb down her belly. His thumb continued its downward path, and he entered her from behind.

Her heart stopped for a second, the connection between them electric. He made love to her, filling up all the empty places in her soul and satisfying every desire.

They lay spent in each other's arms. She couldn't tell if the sweat that dampened her skin was hers or his. She couldn't even tell where her limbs ended and his began as they tangled in the sheets.

He yawned and nibbled the edge of her ear. "Toothbrush."

She wanted to drift off to sleep in his arms, but hygiene called. "I left it—"

A bright, white light started blinking in the corner of the room as a high-pitched whine shattered the air.

Judd bolted upright. "What the hell is going on?"

The acrid scent hit her and she scrambled from the bed, grabbing Judd's arm. "Fire!"

Chapter Twelve

Judd grabbed his jeans from the floor as London flung open her closet door and disappeared into the walk-in. She'd better not be picking out a coordinating outfit.

"London!"

She stumbled out of the closet, clutching some clothes to her chest. "I need to get my father's computer."

He buttoned his jeans and swept his shirt from the floor. He took her by the arm. "We need to get out of here now."

They hit the bottom of the stairs and she pushed him toward the dining area. "Grab the laptop while I put these clothes on."

He snagged the computer from the kitchen table and tucked it under his arm. By the time he returned to the foyer, London had on a pair of sweats and was pulling a sweatshirt over her head.

He stopped her from rushing out the front door, placing his palms against it first. Not feeling any heat, he cracked open the door and stuck his head into the hallway. Gray smoke rolled down the hall from the opposite direction of the stairwell. He stepped out the doorway and pulled London behind him. "Let's head for the stairwell. I have my phone. I'll call nine-one-one."

He yanked open the heavy fire door leading to the stairwell and let it slam behind them. Their bare feet slapped against the metal stairs as they jogged down.

When Judd got through to the emergency line, they informed him that the fire department was already on the way.

They joined other residents of the building in varying states of undress in the stairwell. Nobody seemed to know where the fire had started—but he had a good idea.

If he hadn't been so focused on bedding London, he would've done a better job of securing that unoccupied unit. In fact, he should've stayed there like he'd planned to... until London had curled her arms around him on the bike, pressing her sexy body against his in all the right places. He'd decided then and there he had to make good on the promise between them.

When they hit the lobby, the overnight security guard was already letting the firemen into the building.

One of the firefighters stepped into the middle of the lobby. "Did anyone see anything?"

Judd spoke up. "There's heavy smoke on the top floor of the building from unit 502. It's unoccupied."

The fire captain directed the firemen streaming through the front doors of the lobby. "Fifth floor, unoccupied unit. Everyone out of the building."

The residents shuffled through the doors and Judd kept hold of London's hand.

She pressed her shoulder against his. "Someone set fire to my place. How did they get in?"

"They got in because I was too busy satisfying my own pleasure instead of looking out for you."

She squeezed his hand. "That's ridiculous. It would've been worse if you'd been sleeping in there. Maybe you wouldn't have made it out alive."

"If I'd been sleeping in there instead of in your bed, the

other guy wouldn't have made it out alive. There's a reason why you keep business and pleasure separate."

Tucking her fingers into the waistband of his jeans, she tugged him close. "That's not possible for us and you know it. We're in this together, Judd, now more than ever."

He wrapped his arms around her and held her snug against his body, and that was all the confirmation she needed.

While the firefighters worked upstairs, the residents returned to the lobby, where groups huddled under blankets and sipped hot coffee provided by the security guard.

The fire captain took the elevator down to the lobby, and London pinched Judd's arm and pointed. "That's a good sign."

"Ladies and gentlemen. There was a small blaze in the unoccupied unit on the top floor caused by some faulty wiring in the kitchen. We have it contained, and there's no damage to any of the common areas. I understand the owner of the unit is here, so I may please speak to her? The rest of you can return to your homes."

Judd pushed up from the floor where they'd been curled up beneath a blanket and extended his hand to her.

She grabbed it and he pulled her to her feet, leading her to the fire captain.

"I'm London Breck. I own the unit."

"Ma'am, I'm afraid there's some extensive damage to the place, mostly from the smoke and the CO_2 we used, but we had to make sure it didn't spread to the rest of the building or even the rest of the floor."

"I understand. You said it was electrical?"

"Some wires in the kitchen. It's common, especially in vacant units. You really should think about renting it out and keeping it occupied once you repair it."

"Thanks for the tip."

Judd grabbed her elbow and steered her toward the stairwell. "Can you manage five flights of stairs or do you want to wait for all those people to go up the elevator?"

"I can do stairs." She stopped at the first step and grabbed his arm. "Just so we're clear, we both know that was no accidental electrical fire."

"We're clear."

When they got to her floor, the smell of smoke and flame retardant lingered in the air. They didn't even bother going back to bed. She knew she couldn't sleep. Instead she plopped on the couch, crossing her legs beneath her.

"What was he after this time? Do you think he's trying to kill me?"

"I hate to break it to you, but there are easier ways to do that than setting fire to the unit next to yours. He was trying to drive you out of your place or destroy it."

She smoothed her hands across her father's laptop, which Judd had placed on the coffee table. "Or destroy something in it."

"Back to the laptop?"

"Maybe it wasn't the laptop. Maybe it's something else he thinks I have."

Judd rubbed his eyes. "I want to catch this guy in the act just once. All I need is five minutes alone with him. I'd get some answers."

She ran her hands across the muscles of his shoulders and down his corded arms. "I have no doubt about that, but until then we can do our own investigative work."

"There's just one problem with that."

Was he going to cut her out now? She wouldn't be able to go back to the office and be a good little CEO if he did.

"What's the problem?" She sipped a small breath in and out.

"My temporary crib just got burned out. You don't expect me to bunk next door now, do you?"

She scooted close to him and cupped his bristly jaw with one hand. "You're going to stay here with me."

"After the night we just had?" He cinched her wrist with his fingers. "For a second there, when I smelled that smoke, I thought it was coming from the bed where we'd just sparked a raging inferno."

"It *was* hot."

He shook his head. "I should've been able to control myself. We're both too distracted. We need to be stronger."

"I don't see it like that." She flicked his cheek. "When we connected, I mean really connected, I felt invincible. You don't distract me, Judd Brody. You don't make me weaker. You complete me. You make me stronger."

He loosened his grip and pressed a warm kiss on the inside of her wrist, the pulse in his lower lip matching the beat of her own pulse.

"Let's go to bed and get some sleep. We have a big day ahead of us."

JUDD STUDIED LONDON'S face, illuminated by the late-morning sun he'd allowed to filter through the blinds.

Her words from last night about their connection and completing each other had him rethinking everything. He couldn't lead her on. She expected something from him, something he wasn't capable of giving.

He had a big, gaping hole where his heart was supposed to be. How could he ever give London what she desired? What she deserved?

He touched the edge of her long lashes with his finger-tip. They both might be better off if he backed out now and turned over this job to another professional—a true professional, one who wouldn't allow a pair of long legs and a flash of silver hair to interfere with his work.

She sighed in her sleep and her lush lips parted.

He couldn't leave her now. He'd get to the bottom of who

was threatening her and why, handle it and then convince London she was better off without him.

He could always play on her desire to be the big, important, serious CEO. No CEO worth her salt would be caught dead with a man more comfortable in jeans straddling a Harley than in a Savile Row suit commanding a boardroom.

She had to know she couldn't keep one high-heeled foot in both worlds. He had to convince her.

Her fingers trailed along his bare thigh. "Breakfast in bed? The yummy kind?"

"I'm fresh out of condoms, and we have a lot to do today. I'm going to set up some cameras around here, since the management of this building seems to be delinquent on that score. I need to bring some of my stuff over here, too, if I'm going to be your live-in bodyguard."

"I like the sound of that." Her light touch turned into a caress, and he had to use every ounce of his willpower to break away from her.

"I'm going to take a quick shower and get some errands done before the festivities tonight. Do you need to go into your office today?"

"Yep. I'll be there all day, and we can meet up here to get ready for the benefit."

"Sounds good. I may be in and out of your building today to change the locks next door and to work on the camera coverage."

"You first." She snuggled back under the covers. "There are clean towels in the cabinet in the master bath."

He crossed the room and scooped up his jeans and T-shirt from the chair when he'd tossed them last night. He stepped into the cavernous bathroom and poked his head into the cabinet, which was stocked with thick beige towels and smelled like some kind of flower—roses or lavender. Hell, he didn't know the difference—it smelled sweet.

He snatched a towel and hung it on the rack outside

the rectangular shower encased in glass. Cranking on the water, he stepped into the shower onto the tiles that looked like river rocks.

The warm water hit his chest and steam rose immediately, fogging up the glass. He sluiced water through his hair and lathered it up. Then he squirted some liquid soap into his hands and ran them across his chest, the friction creating fragrant suds. He hoped he didn't end up smelling like a rose after this shower.

A blast of cold air hit his back and he turned right into London's arms.

Running her hands across his chest, she said, "Looks like I'm just in time. Turn around."

What could he do? She was his boss.

He turned and wedged his palms against the tile as the water beat against his side.

His belly tightened as her smooth hands rubbed circles on his back. When she reached his backside and skimmed her fingernails against his skin, he forgot all about professionalism. Forgot about the black hole in his chest. Forgot about leaving her.

Several hours later and in need of another shower, Judd stepped back into the hallway of London's floor and waved his hand at the minuscule camera in the corner. It worked on a motion sensor, so he wouldn't have hours of blank video to stare at. If something moved in this hallway, that camera would pick it up.

He'd crawled around the kitchen of the vacant unit in the wake of the firefighters but hadn't found any evidence to indicate the fire had started from anything other than faulty wiring. Of course, that could be manipulated—and probably had been.

The elevator pinged and his muscles tensed, his hand hovering over the weapon in his shoulder holster.

London stepped off the elevator, the navy blue suit she'd

donned this morning after their steamy shower still crisp and fresh.

She dropped her briefcase and put her hands on her hips. "What a welcome sight you are after the day I just had."

His pulse ratcheted up a few notches. "Anything go wrong?"

"Yes." Her eyes widened and she took a step forward. "Not in that way. Nothing life threatening, unless you count being bored to death."

"More meetings?"

"I think so. I was half-asleep."

"Everyone going to the ballet benefit tonight?"

"Everyone will be there. Why don't we just lock them up in the opera house and question them under a bright light?"

"The ballerinas, too?"

"Can't hurt." She gestured around the hallway. "Did you get all your stuff done?"

"Cameras, check. New locks, check. Clean clothes, check."

"Are you going to wear the tux from the other night?"

"Uh, let me think about that." He wedged a finger on his chin and rolled his eyes to the ceiling. "Yeah, it's the only one I have."

"Okay." She picked up her briefcase and sauntered to her door, key chain ready.

"Why? Something wrong with it?"

"It's fine, just a little tight through the shoulders and back."

"Yeah, well, if I stick out a little tonight among the mon-eyed set, that's a good thing. Don't want any of them getting too comfortable."

She slid her key home and laughed. "That's how I first noticed you the night of the gala. You looked like an alien in that bunch."

He covered her hand as she closed it around the door handle. "I always will, London. I'll never fit in."

The smile died on her lips as she twisted the doorknob and shoved the door open. "I don't want you to."

She showered first, and he left her in peace, although visions of her sleek wet body kept him from concentrating on the TV news.

He showered next, but this time she kept her distance. He had laid out his tux on the bed, and the room was empty when he finished his shower and dressed.

"Are you decent?" She poked her head into the bedroom.

"A little late for that consideration, wouldn't you say?" He leaned into the mirror, his fingers fumbling with the bow tie.

London stepped into the room, tightening the sash on her pink terry-cloth robe, her damp hair streaming down her back. "Let me."

She stood on her tiptoes between him and the mirror and took the bow tie from him as he tilted his chin toward the ceiling. The black band looped around her slim fingers as she tied it into a bow.

"There." She patted her handiwork with two fingers.

"Thanks." He tapped the base of her throat. "Shouldn't you be getting ready, or are you always fashionably late?"

"It doesn't take me long to get ready. I just need to dry my hair, put on makeup and slip into—" she waved her hand at a bag hanging on the door of her closet "—that."

"I'll wait for you downstairs. Do you mind if I take a look at your father's computer?"

Her eyes flicked. "I actually brought it back to the office today. There's a top-notch safe in my father's office. Really, I won't be long. Have a drink or something. You might need it to get through tonight."

Shrugging, he swept his jacket from the bed. "I might just do that."

He draped the jacket over his arm and jogged downstairs, passing the spot where he'd taken her last night. He'd been crazy with desire and a need to possess her after exploring the unit next door. The thought of someone spying on her, watching her through that peephole, had driven him to march back over here and make her his own. As if making love to her could somehow put a force field of protection around her.

Then someone had started that fire.

He crossed over to the wet bar, lifted a few stoppers from some cut-crystal decanters and sniffed the contents. The stuff inside was probably more expensive than the container that held it. Just what he needed.

He picked up two tumblers from the shelf below and filled each one about half-full with the amber liquid from the fanciest decanter. He swirled the booze in his glass and took a sip.

The cognac felt like warm velvet against his tongue. He cupped it there for a second before swallowing it, savoring the smooth taste. His gaze wandered toward London's briefcase on the floor by the coffee table.

He'd thought she'd be gung ho about his suggestion of searching through her father's laptop. She should've left it here for him to take a look at it. He hadn't placed as much importance on the laptop as she had, and maybe she didn't want him to rain on her parade. He'd have to insist they look at it together.

A flash of green from across the room caught his attention, and his head jerked up. He clenched his jaw so it wouldn't fall open and make him look like the village idiot. Not much he could do about the erection he sported.

"You look amazing."

She twirled for him, the skirt of the green mermaid dress flaring at her ankles and the flash of green light around her neck ricocheting across the walls.

"Are you going to be able to walk in that, or do I have to carry you around all night—not that I mind doing that?" He eyed the dress that fit tightly over her slim hips and down her thighs.

"There's lots of wiggle room." She thrust her leg through a slit in the front of the dress.

He leveled a finger at the deep, plunging neckline that almost reached her belly button. "You'd better not wiggle too much."

"Everything's firmly in place."

She cupped her breasts through the silky material of the dress, giving him an even bigger reason not to step out from behind the wet bar.

"And what is that rock hanging between your…uh… assets, there?"

"This little bauble?" She slipped her finger along the chain and lifted the green stone surrounded by diamonds from her chest. "This is an emerald. It has some significance for tonight—a Russian prince gave this emerald to a prima ballerina. One of the ballet dancers tonight is reportedly a descendant of that Russian prince."

"Are you going to give it back to him?"

"Ah, no." She dropped the emerald back against her chest, where it could've cracked her breastbone.

"You're just going to dangle it in front of him?" He'd rather feast his eyes on the creamy breasts cradling the emerald than that cold stone.

Cold. He couldn't believe he'd once figured London Breck for a cold ice princess.

He cleared his throat and tapped the glass. "Cognac?"

"Drop a few ice cubes in there and I'll take a sip." She tilted her head and her hair fanned out over one shoulder. "I thought you were strictly a beer man?"

"Did I say that?" He rolled the glass between his hands. "I prefer it, but hell, if I'm going to hobnob with the fabulously wealthy, I might as well drink like them. Where's the ice?"

"I'll get it from the freezer in the kitchen."

"I'll get it." He stepped around her with the glass in his hand and went into the kitchen. He stuck the cognac beneath the ice dispenser and pressed the lever. Two ice cubes splashed into the liquid and a few droplets hit his wrist.

He sucked it off and handed her the glass. He returned to the wet bar and raised his own. "Here's to getting some answers tonight—either at the soiree or after it."

"I'll drink to that." She tipped her tumbler toward him.

Before they could finish their drinks, a low buzzing sound came from her intercom. She pushed the button and the security guard's voice came through the box. "Ms. Breck, your car's here."

"Thank you. We'll be right down."

Judd said, "Too bad Theodore's not in the driver's seat tonight."

"You got that right. I just hired a service."

"Coat?" He jerked his thumb toward the closet in the foyer.

"I don't have anything that matches this. You'll just have to keep me warm." She winked at him as she swept past him out the door.

Watching her swaying hips, he said, "It didn't stop you from pairing a sparkly black dress with a leather motorcycle jacket before."

"I didn't have you to keep me warm then."

The acrid smell from the fire still lingered in the hallway—a bleak reminder that he could keep London warm, but he'd better keep her safe.

The driver was waiting by the limo and jumped to open the door when he and London stepped onto the sidewalk.

London plucked up the skirt of her dress, fell onto the seat and shimmied to the middle.

Judd ducked into the car and joined her. "I think you'd be more comfortable in the water in that dress than on land."

"I do look like a mermaid, don't I?" She smoothed the material across her lap.

"That was the first thing that came to my mind, except you'd lose that emerald in the ocean."

She plucked it off her chest and cradled it in the palm of her hand. "It belonged to my mother. But let's not dwell on the past."

"I like your past. It's colorful. It's you. Beats mine."

She brushed the back of her hand across his cheek. "I can't imagine. Kids need stability. They need both of their parents."

Her voice quavered in the darkness and he looked at her sharply. She didn't seem as though she would be overly fond of children in general. Did she pity the child he'd been?

He grabbed her hand and kissed her palm. "Don't feel bad for me. My brothers were all right—not exactly a substitute for a mom and a dad, but Sean did the best he could. Eric, too. From all accounts, my old man was strict. With him around, I probably would've turned out completely different."

"So you believe nurture has as much to do with our personalities as nature?"

"I guess so. Look at you."

"Me?"

"You lost your mom at an early age. Maybe with a mother's influence, you wouldn't have been such a hell-raiser, but then, it could just be in your genes." He tugged on a lock of her silky hair. He preferred it like this rather than up in some bun on top of her head.

"People can change."

He rolled his eyes. "Yeah, I know that, Ms. CEO."

The limo rolled to a stop and seconds later, the driver

opened the door for them. "Will you text your departure, Ms. Breck, or do you want me to be here at a specific time?"

"Plan for around midnight, but if you're not here, Mr. Brody will text you."

Other limos and town cars jammed the street in front of the opera house, depositing passengers who glittered from head to toe with jewels.

Not one woman could compare with London.

She took his arm as they ascended the steps, more date than bodyguard. How would Roger react to his presence?

Her cousin Niles greeted them first at the top of the steps. "London, you've outdone yourself. That necklace is the perfect touch. Is that that Kaparov emerald?"

"It is." She squeezed Judd's arm. "Niles knows my mother's jewelry better than I do."

Did he know it and covet it?

"I don't know why you keep insisting on referring to those jewels as your mother's. She left them all to you when she died. They're yours, London."

"Can we talk about this another time, like never?" She waved to a couple, her scowl morphing to a smile. "Are the dancers here yet?"

"I have no clue. I just arrived." Niles arched a brow. "Do you enjoy the ballet, Judd?"

"No."

Niles put one hand into the pocket of his jacket and tipped his nose in the air. "I'm going to mingle. You kids have fun."

As they watched him walk away, Judd leaned close to London's ear. "He knows way too much about your family business."

"That's because he's family."

He nodded toward Wade with a pretty African-American woman. "Does your brother know as much?"

"No. He's on the business side of things only. Dad didn't

include him in the personal details of our lives. His existence was a source of pain for my mother."

"Does he resent that?"

"I doubt it." She tugged on his sleeve. "Come on. I'll introduce you to his wife, Stephanie. She's his polar opposite."

"Hi, Wade. Stephanie, I'm glad you could get away from the kids."

Stephanie smiled and winked at Judd. "You make it sound as if they're holding me captive or something."

Wade nodded curtly at Judd, but Stephanie grasped Judd's hand with both of hers. "Are you going to introduce me to your date, London?"

"This is Judd Brody. Judd, Stephanie Vickers."

Wade rested hand on his wife's shoulder. "I told you, Steph, Mr. Brody is London's bodyguard."

Stephanie's eyes widened. "You never told me London's bodyguard was Judd Brody. I've been following your family's story recently, Judd. Can I call you Judd?"

"Sure."

London leaned in toward her brother. "While we're on the subject, did Dad ever mention Joseph Brody to you, Wade?"

That was one way to get it out in the open. Judd studied Wade's face, but it showed nothing but indifference.

"No." His fingers curled into Stephanie's shoulder. "Steph, we need to say hello to Adam Cantor and his wife."

"If you say so." She kissed London's cheek. "Nice to see you, London, and that dress is fabulous."

"They seem mismatched," Judd said after they moved away.

"Oh, I don't know. It's a case of opposites attracting. She makes him more human."

"And what does he do for her?"

"He's stable, a good provider. He offers her a lifestyle

where she can stay home with their kids. That's important to her."

Judd narrowed his eyes and peered across the crowded lobby. "Looks like my friend got another gig."

"Who do you mean?" She waved and smiled at a few more clusters of people.

"My friend Rick. He's the one who was supposed to be working for Bunny that night." He raised his hand. "He's over there."

"Do you want to talk to him? There are a few rounds I need to make."

"Go ahead. You're staying in this area, right?"

"Yes. I see the dancers by the stairs. I'm going to talk to them."

He watched her join the group of dancers, who were already in costume. Great, he'd have to sit through dancers tiptoeing across the stage.

He shouldered his way through the throng of people to reach Rick and thrust out his hand. "So Bunny gave you another chance, or is it someone else tonight?"

"I'm looking after Bunny." Rick whistled. "I saw your arm candy tonight. Seems like you made out like a bandit."

"London Breck? I'm doing some personal security for her."

"I wouldn't mind doing a little personal security for her." Rick wiggled his eyebrows up and down. "Guess it all worked out for the best."

"What did?"

Bright red suffused Rick's face. "I sort of tricked you, dude."

"Tricked me? What the hell are you talking about?"

"That night I was supposed to work for Bunny? I hadn't really double booked. I got a strange call from a lady the day before the gig."

"Have you been hitting the open bar? What are you

talking about?" Judd's heart had started to thump hard, rattling his rib cage.

"Look, man, I wouldn't have done it, but it was a lady asking, so I didn't see any harm. If I sensed any danger, I never would've done it."

"Rick, dude, would you just spit it out? What are you talking about?"

"The day before that Breck benefit, a lady called me. She said she was a friend of London Breck's and she wanted you two to meet. The whole thing was a setup."

Chapter Thirteen

The blood was thundering against his temples, and his vision blurred. "She wanted me and London to meet?"

"That's what she told me, just a little fun. She offered me money if I would give up the job for Bunny to you."

"You did that?" Judd's hands curled into fists.

"Dude, she offered me a lot of money, and I didn't see the harm in it."

"Really?" Judd had taken a step closer to Rick and loomed over him. "What if it was a setup? What if someone wanted me there to take me out?"

"It was a lady, dude."

"Who was it? What was her name?"

"I don't know. She didn't tell me and we never met. Once I cleared the gig with you and let her know, she left an envelope of cash in my mailbox. End of story."

It was far from the end of the story. Their meeting hadn't been fate, but it had been someone's plan.

"I can't believe you did that, Rick. You compromised my safety."

"Dude—" his gaze tripped over Judd's shoulder "—I think I did you a favor."

Judd could smell London's perfume before she tapped him on the shoulder. "Is this your friend?"

"London, this is Rick Jacobs. Rick, London Breck."

They shook hands. "Good to meet you, London. If this surly SOB ever gets on your nerves, I'm available 24/7."

"But Rick is a careless SOB."

London drew her brows over her nose and looked from him to Rick. "What does that mean?"

"Rick gave up his job with Bunny to me because someone paid him to do so."

"Dude!"

"Really?" London grabbed Rick's hands. "I knew it was all connected."

Rick's eyebrows disappeared in his shock of dishwater-blond hair. "Now I'm confused."

"Good. You deserve to be confused for pulling a stunt like that. Do you have this woman's number?"

"I can probably get it off my cell unless I deleted it. I figured since I didn't hear about your untimely demise at that benefit, she was on the up-and-up." He saluted at Bunny across the room. "I have to get back to work, but I'll find you later and we'll go through my phone."

When the crowd swallowed up Rick, London turned to Judd. "We're more connected than we realized."

"Maybe what our ex-con has to tell me tonight about my father will shed some light on your situation."

"I know it will." Her green eyes sparkled as brilliantly as that emerald around her neck.

His stomach clenched. She wanted in on the meeting tonight and he hadn't figured out yet how he planned to dissuade her, other than tying her up. "London."

She put her finger to her lips. "Listen. The orchestra is tuning up. I'm going to watch the performance. Maybe Rick can check his phone while they're playing."

She slipped away through the crowd, a flash of green darting among a sea of black.

Judd scanned the people moving toward the staircases and elevators like a herd of cows—very well-dressed cows.

He spotted Bunny with enough jewels dripping from her small frame to topple her over sideways. His gaze shifted to Rick hovering behind her.

If Judd had to hazard a guess, he'd bet that Bunny had a greater interest in keeping attractive young men at her beck and call than she did in protecting the wealth of jewelry she sported around her wrists and neck and hanging from her earlobes.

He caught Rick's eye and jerked his thumb toward one of the bars set up in the lobby.

Rick ducked his head and whispered into Bunny's ear. She patted his hand and took the arm of an older gentleman heading into the elevator.

The mass of people had thinned, and Judd strode to the bar and ordered a club soda just as Rick joined him.

"Make that two." Rick pulled his phone from his jacket pocket. "I'm guessing you want that number about now. Do not identify yourself or tell her I told you anything. The money she gave me was supposed to ensure my silence."

"You made an unethical decision by accepting that money."

"Yeah, yeah, tell it to the pop princess and Saudi princes you get to accompany to Hawaii and the French Riviera. Some of us P.I.s are working stiffs who don't get the jobs you do, Brody."

"I am a working stiff."

"Yeah, that's why you're here tonight at this gala."

"As a bodyguard, just like you."

Rick snorted. "Yeah, right. I wish my clients hung on to me the way London Breck hangs on to you—well, if my clients were London Breck."

Judd slammed his glass on the bar. "Just get that number."

Rick skimmed his thumb up and down his phone's display. "Let's see. That would've been almost a week ago, the day before the benefit at the hotel. I got it."

"You're sure? It's a real number, not blocked?"

"I think this is it." He held the phone in Judd's face.

Judd whispered the number several times, and then turned to the woman sipping a pink cocktail next to him. "Ma'am, can I borrow your phone to make a quick call? My battery's dead."

"Of course." She placed her drink on the bar and slipped her hand into her evening bag, pulling out her phone.

When he reached for it, she pulled it back. "I hope you're not calling a friend like—" her gaze roamed up and down his body "—you. My husband is very jealous and likes to check the numbers on my cell."

"I'm calling a woman. It shouldn't cause you any problems." Hell, her husband might've hired him to spy on her in the past.

She dropped the phone in his hand and retrieved her drink, taking a careful sip from the wide rim.

Judd closed his eyes for a few seconds to recall the number and then tapped it into the woman's phone. It rang four times before an answering machine picked up. "Hello. You've reached Bay Realtors, the San Francisco Realtor for all your real estate needs. Our office is closed, but if you'd like to leave a message, please do so at the tone. If you are calling about one of our listings, please leave the address of the property and the name of the Realtor. Thank you and have a great San Francisco Bay day."

When the tone beeped, Judd swallowed and ended the call.

"Well?" Rick took a swig of his water.

"It's a Realtor's office, no individual name. The person who called you could've borrowed a phone there, or could be a customer. Not a lot of help."

"I tried, dude."

Judd slid the cell phone next to the woman's cocktail glass on the bar. "Thank you."

She fluttered her eyelashes. "No problem. Not a fan of ballet?"

"Not really."

"Me, either." She adjusted the bodice of her halter dress, where a diamond almost the size of London's emerald glittered between her ample bosoms. "There's a quiet little alcove downstairs where we could get to know each other better and discuss our mutual dislike of the ballet."

"No, thank you, ma'am." He pushed away from the bar, ignoring Rick's smirk. "I'm working tonight."

She called after him, "You can work for me anytime."

"Haven't lost the old Brody magnetism." Rick punched Judd's shoulder and whistled between his teeth. "That one's ripe for the picking."

"That one's trouble."

"Never stopped you before."

A few hot retorts sprang to his lips, but he swallowed them. Rick had it right. Courting trouble had never stopped him before—before meeting London. Of course, London represented a whole other level of trouble.

He and Rick parked outside the doors to the orchestra level, where he could hear the music swell and fall. A burst of applause erupted and an attendant flung open the doors.

"Short intermission. Do you want to take a seat now?"

"No, thanks." Judd spotted London's gleaming head bobbing as she talked to several people crowded around her. He'd let her do her thing and tell her about the call when she could break away.

As if sensing his scrutiny, she glanced up and met his eyes. She must've read something in his face because she started to shuffle down her row of seats.

Rick clapped him on the back. "Duty calls. I'll catch up with you later."

As Rick melted into the crowd, Judd turned to watch London's approach. She could barely move three feet without someone stopping her to say a word or two, touching her arm, giving her a hug.

She drew people to her. They gravitated toward her as if to bask in her light, but they didn't stand in awe of her. They acted so familiar with her. Each and every one saw her as a friend, a confidante. She had the knack of making a person feel important, noticed.

Interpersonal skills like that didn't belong in a boardroom, behind a desk. Couldn't she see that she had something so much more important than a head for business?

When she reached him, she hooked her arm in his. "Sorry that took so long. All those people knew my father. I hadn't seen most of them since the memorial service and funeral."

She tapped his glass of club soda. "Is that water? I could use one of those."

"It's club soda. Hold it for me and I'll get you one." Once he'd gotten her drink, he turned back, but he could barely see her through the clutch of people hovering around her, including her cousin and Richard Taylor.

He hung back. They couldn't discuss business with all those folks listening in.

"I heard you were working for London."

Judd jerked his head toward the man to his left, who looked familiar to him. A former client? "And you are?"

"I'm sorry. I thought you would've recognized me since we met once or twice." The man's dark eyes assessed Judd as he stuck out his hand. "I'm Captain Les Williams. I work with your brother Sean."

Judd transferred London's glass to his left hand and gripped the captain's hand. "Good to meet you."

"Do you know when Sean is returning? We need him—damned good detective. Runs in the family."

"I don't know when Sean's coming back."

The crowd around London had thinned, and she was signaling to him. "If you'll excuse me."

"Of course. Who wouldn't rather be talking to that young lady?"

Judd hadn't even reached her side, and she broke away from the few remaining people in the group, including her cousin, who glared at him.

She grabbed his hand and pulled him into a corner. "Did Rick still have the number on his phone?"

"He did and I called it."

Her eyes widened as she squeezed his hand. "And?"

"It went to a real estate office—Bay Realtors. Just a generic message, no specific agent." He handed her the glass. "Your club soda."

"Oh." She wrapped her hand around the glass and gave him his. "It could be anyone—a client, a Realtor's friend, even a stranger."

"My thoughts exactly."

She tossed her head, flicking her hair over her shoulder. "But we can always look up the office and visit it in person, ask around."

"We could do that." He jerked his thumb toward the opera house, where the orchestra was striking up a few chords. "Another round?"

"It's very brief. Did you get something to eat yet?"

"There's food?" His stomach rumbled at the thought.

"I thought the caterer was going to start setting up during the first performance. You should check downstairs and eat something before the hordes descend. Nothing more frightening than a bunch of rich people stampeding for free food."

He traced his finger around the rock resting against the smooth skin of her chest. "You act like you're not one of them."

"Oh, I'm one of them. The trick is not acting like one of them." She dropped her long lashes over her eyes, handed the glass back to him after one sip and grabbed the arm of a passing octogenarian. "Oscar, so glad you could come out tonight. I hope you plan to leave a big check before you leave."

The old man chuckled and patted London's hip. "Only if you sit with me, dear."

Judd shook his head, downed his drink and then hers. Then he jogged downstairs to get first dibs on the food.

Through the next dance performance, Judd did justice to the free food and nursed another club soda. London hadn't been kidding about the stampede. The line for the fancy grub snaked downstairs from the lobby of the opera house to the restaurant on the floor below. He watched London as she barely took a bite of food, weaving through the lines, smiling and glad-handing. She'd probably raised a half a mil for the arts in the past half hour alone.

Turning his wrist, he checked his watch—fifteen minutes to showtime. Maybe he could sneak out of here for the meeting while London continued her fund-raising.

"Are you sure you're doing your job, Brody?"

Judd turned slowly and shifted his gaze down slightly to meet the cold eyes of Richard Taylor.

"London and I can't be joined at the hip at a function like this. I'm keeping my eye on her…sir."

"Joined at the hip." He stroked his chin. "That's an interesting image. It's a common one, but when is any one of us really ever joined to the hip of another?"

"Sir?" Judd's brows collided over his nose. What the hell was this reptilian SOB going on about?

"I actually wasn't referring to this event, Brody. I heard about the fire on London's floor last night."

Judd set his jaw and stared at Taylor without blinking.

He wouldn't give him the satisfaction of asking him how he knew about the fire. Besides, he needed to get rid of him.

Taylor blinked and glanced down. "I know people in the building."

Judd still didn't make a response or move a muscle.

Taylor coughed. "Just want to make sure London's okay. Unlike some, I applauded her decision to hire a… bodyguard."

"Enjoying yourself, Richard?" London stepped between them as if sensing the tension. "Where's Roger tonight?"

"A little under the weather." He held up his index finger and clicked his tongue. "You could deliver the cure if you accepted his marriage proposal."

London playfully grabbed his finger. "You know that's not going to happen, Richard. We would be just awful together and you know it."

"I'd love to have you as my daughter, London."

"The two of us can play pretend father-daughter without the marriage." She released his finger. "Now, if you'll excuse us, Judd and I have a little business to discuss. Don't forget your contribution tonight."

"I thought the ticket *was* the contribution."

"You know me better than that, Richard." She nudged Judd in the back and he nodded at Taylor.

She whispered, "It's midnight already. People are going to start leaving once they've eaten their fill."

"Stay here, London. I can do this on my own."

"I know you can, but I want to be with you."

He ran a hand down her bare arm. "You don't have a coat. Who knows if the guy's even there. We might have to wait out in the cold for him."

"I can fix that." She stopped at the coat check and hunched over the counter. "I'm so sorry. I forgot my ticket, but I see my cloak right there, the black one."

"No problem." The woman handed over the cloak and London slipped her some cash.

"I hope you plan to return this." He snatched the cloak from her arm and draped it over her shoulders, pulling the neck closed over the sparkling emerald.

"Of course. Now let's blow this joint."

"Have you noticed that you start using what you believe is gangster slang whenever we're about to do a little investigating?"

She emitted a very ungangster-like giggle and tucked her hand in his pocket. "May as well get into the spirit of things."

He took her shoulders, spinning her around to face him. "This isn't a joke, London. It's not one of your madcap adventures. You've been the victim of some crazy stuff this past week, and a man was murdered and left for you to discover. You do exactly as I say. Got it?"

Her eyes had gotten bigger and bigger with every word of his tirade and she nodded. "I didn't mean to make a joke about it. I—I mean, I haven't forgotten Griff or Theodore. I know it's serious, Judd."

He kissed her forehead. "Let's be careful."

Taking her hand, he tucked her against his side, and the silk of the cloak rustled as it brushed against him.

The night air felt refreshing after the warmth of the opera house. He rubbed his eyes and took a deep breath of cool air. They crossed the street and circled around to the back of the symphony hall, London's heels clicking on the sidewalk beside him.

He leaned in close. "I have my gun in my shoulder holster. If anything funny happens, duck on my word."

"Got it." She whispered in his ear. "What word?"

"Duck."

They reached the corner of the building and he turned first, keeping London behind him. His nostrils flared at the smell of cigarette smoke wafting toward them. Then he spotted the pinpoint of red light in the darkness.

He took one step toward it and cupped his hand around his mouth. "It's Brody. Walk this way."

A dark shape shoved off the wall of the building and the cigarette sailed into the gutter.

The man strolled toward them, taking his time. Just as the gas station attendant had mentioned, the stranger had a cap pulled low on his face. He kept to the shadows of the building and stopped about five feet away from them. "You alone?"

Judd recognized the voice from the phone call. "I'm with a friend."

"Cops?" The man's body jerked.

"No cops." London stepped out from behind Judd. "Just me."

"London Breck." The man laughed until he started hacking.

London exchanged a look with Judd. "That's right. Is that okay?"

He waved a hand and then shoved it into his pocket, withdrawing a pack of cigarettes, crinkling the plastic that encased the box. He shook one out. "Smoke?"

"No, thanks." Judd shifted his weight to his other foot since the leg felt heavy—too much standing around. "Get to the point."

"You know your old man's partner was killed in a shoot-out, right?"

Judd hunched his shoulders. "Yeah—a meeting a snitch set up that went south."

"That snitch didn't kill Rigoletto."

"He was tried and convicted."

"He was set up—sort of."

"How is someone sort of set up?" Judd blinked his dry eyes. That cigarette smoke was getting to him.

The man tapped his cigarette on his wrist and stuck it between his lips. "He agreed to the setup."

London's cloak rustled beside Judd, and he pressed his hand against the small of her back.

"Why would he do that?"

"Lots of reasons that aren't important now. Don't you want to know *why* he was set up? That's the important stuff."

"Okay, shoot."

The man held up his hands. "I ain't armed, boss."

"Go on."

"The cop that was gunned down, Rigoletto? He knew somethin', him and your old man."

Judd's heart thudded against the holster strapped across his chest. "What did they know?"

"That—" the man spit out grains of tobacco "—I can't tell you."

"How do you know the shoot-out was a setup?"

"I shared a cell with Otis Branch—the snitch. He told me someone hired him to take out both cops, but he only got one."

Judd sucked in a breath, which only made his mouth drier. "There was a hit put out on my father and his partner?"

"That's right, but Otis missed Brody. When he saw what went down with Brody about six months later, he figured they'd gotten him another way."

Judd's head pounded, and each thud let loose an explosion of pain. He rubbed his heavy eyes.

London gave him a sharp glance and spoke up. "It couldn't have been Russell Langford, the real Phone Book Killer, who set up Detective Brody. Why would he have any interest in Joe Rigoletto?"

The man clicked a lighter and the flame illuminated his face from below, giving him a ghoulish look.

Judd almost laughed but felt London's piercing stare. He reached out and held up the wall of the symphony hall with his hand.

The man lit his cigarette and took a long drag.

The smoke made Judd dizzy, and he propped a shoulder against the building.

"That's the point. Russ Langford was the Phone Book Killer, but someone besides Langford was setting up Brody. That whole sideshow was just a gift to Langford."

London squeezed his arm through his jacket and it felt so good. Lead weights tugged at his eyelids. He just wanted to find a warm, comfortable bed with London curled up next to him.

"Did Otis ever tell you who hired him?"

"Said he didn't know, but they paid him a lot of money, which he stashed away for his wife and daughter."

London looked at him with raised eyebrows. Was she expecting something from him?

She sighed and asked, "Why didn't he say anything when he was arrested? He just took the fall."

"That's what he got paid to do. He figured if these people could arrange the execution of a cop, they'd have no problem taking him out, or his family. He did his time and his wife got the dough. It's not as if Otis was any stranger to life in the big house."

The man's words rushed through Judd's head. He tried to make sense of them, but they tumbled one after the other.

"That's all I gotta say." He shrugged off the wall. "Thought Brody here would wanna know."

He hesitated and took a pull on his smoke.

Interesting. Or it would be interesting if he weren't so damned tired.

London broke away from his side and fished in her evening bag. She took several steps toward the man, and Judd tried to lift his arm to stop her. She shouldn't get so close.

But his arm wouldn't obey the command from his brain.

London murmured something to the man and he turned and sauntered down the street, his lit cigarette swinging at his side, before disappearing behind the building.

"Judd!" Her fingers dug into his shoulders and she shook him. "Are you okay? You just stopped talking and you look like you're about to topple over."

"Sick." His tongue felt five sizes too big for his dry mouth.

She took his arm. "Our car should be waiting in front of the opera house. If not, I'll text our driver. Just hang on to me."

He laid an arm heavily across her shoulders, but didn't want to lean on her. What if they both fell down? He could fall on top of her—in a fountain. Naked. The laugh that clawed its way up his throat sounded more like a bark.

She stumbled beneath his weight as they made it back to the front of the opera house. A few people littered the steps of the building and the sidewalk, but he couldn't think of anything to say to them.

"Your car, Ms. Breck."

"Thank you. Please hurry. Mr. Brody is ill."

Was he? When did that happen? He couldn't be ill. He was on a job. He had to protect London.

Rough hands grabbed him and bundled him into the back of the limo, and he slumped against London, who was already sitting on the leather seat.

"Hey, be careful. He's not well." She pressed her cool hand against his forehead as the door slammed after them.

He licked his lips. "Water. Give me water."

The car roared to life, throwing him to the other side of the backseat, his head hitting the window. A crack of pain splintered his skull and he blinked. "Water."

He heard the crack of a plastic lid on a bottle, and then

London held it to his mouth. He sealed his lips around the rim and chugged it so fast it ran down his chin.

"Judd!"

He sat up. "More water."

The fog in his head loosened, and he tensed every one of his muscles. He knew how to get out of this. He had to get out of this.

London turned toward him, another bottle of water clutched in her hand. This time he took it from her and downed it.

"Why are you so thirsty?" Her wide eyes glimmered in the darkness of the car. "What's wrong?"

"I've been drugged."

Chapter Fourteen

London's heart flip-flopped, and she stretched out her hand for the call button.

"Don't." Judd circled his fingers around her wrist and jerked her arm down.

"If you've been drugged, you need to go to the emergency room."

He crouched down in the seat and shook his head while reaching inside his jacket. He mumbled a curse. "He took my weapon."

Adrenaline spiked through her body, and she grabbed the seat, her fingernails digging into the soft leather. "Who? The driver?"

"Yeah. It's going to be okay. I didn't finish the last club soda—it tasted funny." He tossed the empty bottle to the floor of the car. "Another water."

Her hand shook as she offered him another plastic bottle. "Why would someone drug you?"

"To get to you."

Her eyes darted to the dark privacy glass that shielded them from the driver. "What are we going to do?"

"Since I don't have my weapon or any way to get to the driver, we're going to have to exit this car."

She swallowed, pulling the borrowed cloak up to her chin. "While it's moving?"

"Do you prefer we wait until he takes us to some location not of our choosing and delivers us to the person who planned this abduction?"

"Abduction?"

"That's what this is, London. Whether they plan to kill me first before we arrive or off me once we get there, they want you." He tipped the rest of the water down his throat and wiped his mouth with the back of his hand.

"You're in no condition to jump from a moving car."

"On the plus side, I probably won't feel a thing when I land. There's a reason drunk drivers never seem to get badly injured in accidents—their bones are like rubber, and that's how I feel."

"I wondered what was going on with you when we were talking to our informant. He said some pretty explosive things that barely got a reaction from you."

"First things first. We need to get out of this car the minute it slows down—while we're still in the city, while there are still traffic signals." His fingers curled around the door handle.

"What if he locked us in back here?" Her teeth chattered and she covered her mouth with one hand.

"I don't think so. He figures I'm going to be knocked out in several minutes, and you're more likely to ask him to take me to the emergency room than to catapult from the car and leave me." He narrowed his eyes at her. "Would you?"

She smiled behind her hand. "What would be the fun in that?"

"Keep this cloak wrapped around you." He tweaked the material with his thumb and forefinger. "It'll restrict your movement, but you don't have much mobility in that dress anyway, and the cloak will protect you if he takes off and you fall out of the car."

"We need your motorcycle helmet."

"We need a lot of things." He squeezed her knee. "Hang

on to me when I give the word. I can break your fall if I have to."

"Judd."

"Yeah?"

"I'm scared."

"Piece of cake. The driver's already hit a few red lights. Now that we're ready, we're going to take advantage of those. If he sees the alert for the open door, he might try to take off. Don't let that deter you. Jump and clear the car—moving or not."

She dipped her chin. "Got it."

London held her breath. She scooted even closer to Judd, pressing her thigh against his, clutching his arm with one hand.

The heavy tint on the windows obscured their location, but the car still trundled along surface streets. Once they hit the freeway, if that was where he was headed, they wouldn't have a chance.

The limo slowed, and Judd poked her leg. The car idled.

"Now!" Judd threw himself against the door, pulling her with him.

As predicted, the driver stomped on the gas and the car lurched forward with one of her legs still inside.

Judd yanked her free and they both stumbled into the street.

Headlights blinded her. A horn blared. A set of brakes squealed.

"He's stopping." Judd grabbed her hand and headed down the street, threading his way through traffic as drivers yelled and honked at them.

He shouted above the din, "We want to stay in public view so he won't take a shot at us or try to run us down."

London stole a peek over her shoulder. "He's on the phone."

"Probably giving his boss the bad news. Keep walking."

They escaped the traffic in one piece and turned down a side street, where a few bars bustled with business.

He pulled her through the first door. "We're going to get a taxi back to Nob Hill."

Fifteen minutes later, London closed her eyes in the backseat of a taxi heading home. "I don't understand what just happened."

Judd put a finger to his lips and then pressed it against hers.

They didn't utter another word until she shut the door to her place and locked it. She stood with her back pressed against the door. Then her knees weakened and she folded at the waist.

Judd was beside her in a heartbeat, catching her in his arms. He scooped her up and cradled her against his chest as if she were a kitten instead of a five-foot-ten-inch woman with gangly arms and legs.

He carried her into the great room and settled her before the fireplace. He dragged an ottoman to her back and she leaned against it while he hunched forward and started the gas to light the logs in the fireplace.

"Do you want another cognac? Just sip it for your nerves."

"Sure." She drew her knees to her chest and wrapped her arms around her legs. "Are you all right? Shouldn't you go to the emergency room?"

He poured from the decanter they'd sampled earlier in the evening. "I think it was a little codeine, that's it. I recognized the effects, and once I realized what had happened I was able to deal with it."

"It was someone in the opera house, someone at the gala."

"Someone you know."

She stretched her chilled fingers to the dancing flames. "Do you think whoever it was knew about our meeting?"

"I don't think so, and that's probably what saved me. If I'd been drugged and then packaged into that limo right away, I probably would've passed out before I knew what hit me. Instead we walked outside. The cool air combated some of the effects of the drug."

"If you hadn't acted so quickly, who knows where I'd be right now? Who knows where you'd be?"

"I should've realized something was up when that club soda left a funny taste in my mouth." He loosened the cloak at her throat. "Distracted. I'm too damned distracted to do my job."

"Stop." She slapped at his hands. "You saved me again. If that's you distracted, then I'm not sure I could handle your intensity undistracted."

He opened the cloak and she shrugged out of it. He draped it over the arm of the couch. "Is that poor woman ever going to get her cape back?"

"After I dry-clean it." She flicked the straps of her dress off her shoulders. "Are we going to call the police and report the limo driver?"

"Did you get his name? License number of the car? What exactly are we going to report? He picked us up and was driving us home."

"Y-you were drugged?"

"And how do I prove that? I'm telling you, it was codeine, a common enough drug."

Sighing, she hooked her little finger in the strap of her shoe and pulled it off her foot. "Were you clearheaded enough to hear what our ex-con had to say?"

"I heard, I comprehended the words, but I haven't been able to get my head around them yet."

"He said the shooting of your father's partner was planned, and someone intended the same fate for your dad, too."

"But Otis missed, so someone set my father up to take

the fall for those murders to get him out of the way or shut him up."

"That's the gist of it—and it worked."

"But shut him up about what? Did the guy mention that?"

"He didn't know. Otis didn't know, but when all that stuff started coming down on Joey Brody, Otis figured it was part of the same plan he'd been involved with."

"It's crazy." Judd pinched the bridge of his nose, closing his eyes. "I need to tell my brothers."

"My father knew."

Judd opened one eye. "Knew what?"

"He knew about the setup of your father and his partner. That's how he knew Joey Brody was innocent."

"Do you know what you're saying?"

"My father was a tough businessman. As far as I know, he was an ethical one, but somehow, some way, he had knowledge of what went down twenty years ago."

"And someone doesn't want you to find out what that was."

"That's it, Judd." She sat up, curling her legs beneath her. "There's someone worried about exposure—the murder of a cop, the obstruction of a police investigation of a serial killer, the planting of evidence."

"Driving of another cop to suicide."

"Do you think he knew? Do you think your father realized what was going on?"

"If he did, why didn't he just expose the perpetrators? Why jump off a bridge?" He smacked a fist into his palm.

"I don't know, but maybe once we find the proof, you can get some answers. Someone is trying very hard to protect the lies of the past."

"Who has the most to lose? Richard Taylor has been with your father from the beginning, hasn't he?"

"Pretty much."

"I'd like to have a look at your father's computer. If he went to such great lengths to hide it, there has to be a good reason." Judd peeled off his jacket and dropped it onto the chair.

London sucked in her bottom lip. Her father hadn't hid his laptop because of those pictures, unless he'd wanted to hide the pictures from her. No. He'd told her the location of the laptop, showed her how to get to it.

Through half-closed eyes, she watched Judd strip down to his undershirt and slacks. She didn't need to keep secrets from him. Showing him the pictures on her father's laptop might be the perfect way to tell him. If he judged her and she lost him...well, she'd never had him anyway.

Nobody owned Judd Brody and nobody ever would. He'd do as he pleased. Even now he preferred to call in his brothers rather than put forth an effort for a father he'd dismissed as weak.

Would he dismiss her as weak, too?

"Yeah, we'll look at his computer tomorrow. Like I said, I brought it back to the office, thought it might be safer there with all the stuff going on in this building."

He slid behind her, pulling her back between his legs. Then he kissed her neck. "We'll hit the real estate office first, and then go to your office for the laptop."

The warmth from the fire on her face and the warmth from his kisses on the nape of her neck soaked through the rest her body, and she felt as drugged as if someone had spiked her drink, too.

She curled her arms around his legs and rubbed her hands along the insides of his thighs, crumpling the smooth material of his slacks.

His legs tightened around her and his hands slipped beneath her low-cut dress to cup her breasts. When his thumbs toyed with her nipples, she melted against him.

And then he took her, and the fear and tension of the

evening drifted away. Maybe nobody would ever own Judd Brody, but Judd Brody owned her—mind, body and soul.

THE NEXT MORNING, London climbed on the back of the Harley in her pantsuit, feeling right at home. Judd hadn't bothered to exchange his jeans for a suit today, and he'd replaced the weapon the limo driver had taken from him last with another gun from his small arsenal.

They careened through the streets, leaving Nob Hill for the Sunset where Bay Realtors had an office—the same office that Judd had called last night.

When they reached the realty office, London slid from the bike and Judd slotted it into a parking space. He locked the helmet on the side of the bike and slicked back his hair.

She put a hand on his arm as they crossed the street. "Remember. We're not going to barge in there demanding answers. We play it by ear."

"I do this for a living, lady, and sometimes demanding answers is the way to go."

A bell jingled on the door when they entered the realty office and a man and a woman with their heads together, huddled over a desk, both glanced up.

The small office gave London hope. This didn't look like the type of office where strangers roamed in and out using the telephone. Of course, the caller could've been a client.

The two Realtors kept talking, and Judd whispered in her ear, "Doesn't look like either one of them recognizes us or is surprised to see us."

The man straightened up first and put on his best Realtor's smile. "Good morning. What can I do for you?"

Showtime. London cleared her throat. "We're interested in this area and were wondering if you have any listings."

The man made a detour to a desk and swiped a binder from the corner of it before approaching them. "Certainly. I'm Jonathan Quick, and you are?"

"I'm Connie and this is my husband, J-Jim." They hadn't decided on pseudonyms, but Constance was her middle name and Jim had a nice, generic ring to it. And of course, they had to be husband and wife. After the lovemaking they'd shared last night, anything else would be indecent.

"Connie, Jim." Jonathan shook her hand, but Judd had turned away and was strolling toward a rack of flyers.

"We have all our listings over there, but I have the Sunset ones in this book." He patted the white three-ring binder in his hand. "House? Town house? Condo? The Sunset has them all and parking to boot."

"We're looking for a detached single-family home."

"We have several of those." Jonathan placed the binder on a table and flipped it open. He shifted his gaze to Judd, now standing back and staring at some banner on the wall. "Sir, would you like to have a look with your wife? If anything interests you, I'd be happy to take you out for a showing."

Judd pointed to a sign hanging above a desk, crepe-paper streamers on either side of it. "Who's Cynthia?"

"What?" Jonathan's brow wrinkled and he darted a glance at London.

"Cynthia." Judd leaned forward and tapped the sign so that it swayed over the desk. "It says, 'Welcome back, Cynthia.' Is she an agent here?"

"Uh, yes. Cynthia Phelps. Do you know her?"

London took a few steps toward Judd and could feel the tension vibrating from his tightly coiled body. What was he getting at? Was he just fishing?

"I know someone who knows her. She just got out of the hospital, didn't she?"

London's breath quickened. Did Judd know something?

Jonathan joined them, the binder held open in his hands. "She did."

Judd turned, a fake smile on his face. "Is she here?"

Jonathan's shoulders sagged with the realization he might be losing some customers to Cynthia. "She's not here. Actually, she's taking some time off. She left town. Didn't Cynthia leave town, Lori?"

The woman called from her desk. "Yes. She's taking a break for a while."

Jonathan blew out a breath and hugged his binder. "She'll be gone for some time."

"But she was here." Judd flicked the welcome-back banner with his finger. "She came back to the office."

"Yes." Jonathan cocked his head. "We had a little homecoming party for her when she got out of the hospital. Did you speak with Cynthia before? Had she shown you any properties? Because I can pick up where she left off."

"Was she in the office last week?"

"Sir." Jonathan placed the binder back on the edge of the desk and folded his hands in front of him. "Cynthia is not here, but I can help you with your needs."

"She was here last week, wasn't she?"

The question sounded innocent enough, and Judd's voice, low and smooth, didn't contain a hint of a threat or violence, yet Jonathan's eyes bulged from their sockets and he stammered.

"I—I'm going to have to call the police if you don't leave."

"The police?" London stepped between the two men. "There's no need for that. My husband knows Cynthia and thought we could work with her. That's all."

Lori had risen from her desk, clutching her phone. "Why are you asking about Cynthia? She's been through enough."

Judd held up his hands. "I know. I know she has. My brother told me what happened to her. Ryan Brody's my brother, the guy who found her that day and helped her. I'm sorry. I didn't realize she worked here, and when I saw her name it sort of jogged my memory. My brother would want to know that Cynthia's okay. That's all."

London looked from Judd to the two Realtors, not knowing what to believe. Where had this all come from?

Jonathan leaned against the desk and licked his lips. "She's okay. That's all we can tell you."

"Fair enough. I'll let my brother know." He took London's arm and steered her out of the office with two pairs of eyes burning into their backs.

Judd marched her across the street, and when they hit the sidewalk, she jerked her arm away from his hold. "What the hell was that all about? Who is Cynthia? Was all that true about Ryan? What happened to her?"

Looking up and down the street, Judd said, "We need to find a place to talk."

"Coffee place around the corner. I saw it when we rode up."

They found the coffeehouse and grabbed a table by the window after placing an order.

"This is crazy." Judd ran his hands through his hair.

She snapped her fingers in front of his face. "Let me in on the crazy."

"Cynthia Phelps, aka Cookie Crumb, was a hooker who knew my father twenty years ago."

London widened her eyes.

"Not that way. He'd arrested her pimp or something. Anyway, Cookie was the last person to see my father alive. She saw him jump from the Golden Gate Bridge."

"What?"

"Ryan looked her up when he and Kacie Manning were working on that book together. They talked to her once, and when they went back to see her, someone had beaten her to a pulp. She went into a coma."

"And you think Cynthia's the one who called Rick and bribed him to give that job with Bunny to you?"

"It's obvious, isn't it? Bay Realtors didn't ring a bell with me, but Ryan told me Cynthia was a Realtor and she'd been attacked at a house she was showing in the Sunset. When I saw that sign with her name, it clicked."

"Why would Cynthia do that?"

"Ryan felt that Cynthia knew something. She was too afraid to talk to him and Kacie, and then someone made sure she couldn't talk to them."

"Did she contact Ryan when she came out of her coma?"

"No. Ryan kept calling the hospital until one day he called and they told him she'd been released. The police had spoken to her, but she claimed she couldn't identify her assailant."

The barista called out their names and Judd jumped up to get their drinks.

London took a sip of her coffee and then traced around the edge of the lid. "Instead of telling you what she knows about your father, she arranged to throw us together. That way nobody needs to know she talked to you…or me."

"Dr. Patrick, Cynthia Phelps, Marie Giardano—anyone who knows anything about what happened twenty years ago is a target."

"Who are Dr. Patrick and Marie Giardano?"

"Dr. Patrick was the department psychologist who saw my father after his partner was killed, which we now know was a setup. Before Sean had an opportunity to question him, he had a heart attack and died."

London gasped. "These people are serious. And Marie?"

"She's the longtime records clerk at the department, friends with both my mom and dad back in the day. Any time any of my brothers came around to request the old files to look into the case, she got very nervous, until she just disappeared a few months ago."

"Is she…?"

He lifted his shoulders. "We don't know. She took off

with her purse and passport, packed a bag, and disappeared. I hope to God she's okay and just keeping a low profile until this business all blows over."

"When will that be?" London bit the tip of her fingernail, holding her breath.

"When we solve the mystery and find out what happened twenty years ago. You're not going to be safe until that time, either. Someone out there is always going to be worried about what your father told you or what he left for you to discover."

"He should've just come clean instead of leaving me cryptic notes from the grave."

"He had to have known that he was putting you in danger."

"Wouldn't be the first time my father failed me."

"Join the club."

She covered his hand. "Your father didn't fail you, Judd. He got caught up in something that spiraled out of his control. His partner was murdered, he was being set up as a serial killer—maybe he thought he'd spend the rest of his life in prison for crimes he never committed."

"So you kill yourself? You give up?" He rubbed the hard line of his jaw. "It can't be that easy to set someone up for crimes he didn't commit, unless…"

"Unless what?"

"Unless you're privy to information and resources that would allow you to do something like that."

"Like the police?"

Their eyes met and London's heart hammered so hard she thought it might jump out of her chest onto the table.

Judd nodded. "And the police commission."

"We need to go through my father's files on the laptop, and, Judd—" she tapped the back of his hand with her fingertips "—we're not alone."

"What does that mean?"

"Think about it. Cynthia successfully engineered a meeting between us and someone left that newspaper clipping on your bike. Someone in the know wants us to find the truth. That ex-con stepped forward. Even my father is trying to speak out."

"Then let's go search that laptop."

London hugged Judd around the waist all the way back to the financial district. Whatever happened between them once this was all over, she'd have no regrets. She loved Judd, but she recognized a fellow free spirit when she encountered one. If he went his own way in the end, she could live with it. She'd loved and lost before. It had left a gouge in her heart, but she'd survived it.

He parked in front of the building and they took the elevator up to the BGE offices. London waved at Celine in the outer office.

"I wasn't sure you'd be in today, London. Do you want me to schedule any meetings for you while you're here?"

"No. Judd and I are going to do some work in my office for a while."

"Should I hold your calls? Someone's been trying to reach you all morning, some guy from the Global Giving Foundation."

"You don't have to hold my calls. Put him through when he calls again. That's one of my favorite charities."

"I will. He's been trying just about every hour."

Judd mumbled, "He must really want your money."

"Thanks, Celine." London snapped the door to the office closed. "I don't mind. It's one of the good charities—low overhead, very few administrators, does a lot for kids around the world. It's easy to get people to donate to a cause like that."

"You—" he kissed her on the tip of her nose "—could get people to donate money for snowboards in the Sahara Desert."

"It's easy to get other people's money for causes. Besides, you never know when you might need a snowboard in the desert." She rolled the leather chair to the side and ducked under the desk.

"What are you doing under there?"

"There's a floor safe under the desk. That's where my dad stashed his laptop."

"There's gotta be something more on there than company financials if he went to that much trouble to conceal it."

"That's what I think. That's what I've been telling you." She pulled out the laptop and stationed it on the desk. She slid a glance toward Judd as he pulled up a chair. She could show him the pictures after they went through the rest of her father's files.

She attached a mouse to the side of the laptop and powered on the computer. "I already searched for *Brody, police commission, Phone Book Killer.*"

"Let me have a look at some of the folders and see if anything jumps out at me. Also, if the file or folder doesn't have that specific name, the search may not find those terms in the text. There's a program you can install to block that kind of text search."

"You see? That's why I need your help with this."

They worked side by side, heads huddled together over the laptop. A lot of the files they went through were duplicates of the ones on her father's desktop work computer.

"I don't know." She massaged her temples. "Maybe he just used this as a backup in case the other one went down."

"You already have an automatic backup on the desktop computer. I checked that out when you were in the board meeting."

The telephone on the desk buzzed, and London pressed a button. "Yes?"

"It's that man again from Global Giving."

"I'll take it. I could use a break anyway." The line clicked once and London punched the speaker button while she drew her hands across her face. "Hello? This is London Breck."

An electronically altered voice intoned over the line, "And this is your guardian angel."

She dropped her hands. "Excuse me? Are you calling from Global Giving?"

"I'm calling to give you a piece of advice, London."

Judd's entire frame went rigid beside her.

"Who is this? What are you talking about?"

"I think you know what I'm talking about. I've been trying to get this message to you ever since your father died."

"What do you want? Just come out with it. What is it you want from me?"

"I want you to keep your mouth shut, go about your business and spend your billions of dollars on shoes and trips to the French Riviera."

"You don't want me taking over as CEO of Breck Global Enterprises?"

"I don't give a damn what you do, just stop looking into the Brody case. Everyone knows Brody's innocent now, so drop it."

"Why was he set up? Why was his partner murdered?"

The man on the phone whistled and it sounded like a buzz saw. "You know a lot, don't you? That's why it's time to stop looking for Operation Phoenix. Is Brody with you now?"

She glanced at Judd and he shook his head.

"No."

The man chuckled. "We could've settled this with you a long time ago if my guys had been able to get close to you, but Brody prevented that from happening. Relentless—just like his old man. You never should've hired Judd Brody.

You hired him to protect you, and he ended up putting you in more danger."

Judd's hand jerked and the mouse slipped from the desk.

"Well, I did hire him, and he's going to continue to protect me from your goons, and we're not going to stop. We're not going to stop until we find out what happened twenty years ago."

Judd had retrieved the mouse and was busy tapping the keyboard and clicking through files.

The man's voice sliced through the line like a cold blade. "Oh, but you are going to stop, London, or you're going to be very sorry."

"Let's see, you tried to snatch me twice, broke into my place, set fire to the unit next door, beat up my driver and killed a security guard at my building. I'm not quitting."

"Maybe we can't get to you as long as Brody is in the picture, but we can get to others."

A chill snaked up her spine. "What others?"

"Check your cell phone, London."

She scrambled for her purse and pulled out her phone. A text message with an attachment had come through. Judd hovered over her shoulder, and with trembling fingers she tapped the message to open it, and then tapped the picture attached to the message.

Maddie's face filled the screen. They had her daughter.

"Just one other, London, and we've already done it. We have your daughter, and we're prepared to do whatever it takes to stop you."

Chapter Fifteen

London choked and lunged for the phone. "What have you done with my daughter? Where is she?"

The line had gone dead, and Judd raked a hand through his hair as if to clear the confusion in his brain. A daughter? London had a daughter?

Once she realized her tormenter had hung up, she grabbed the phone and threw it off the desk. She screamed and pushed the laptop, but Judd collected her hands in his.

"Shh. It's going to be okay."

"Is everything okay, London?" Celine tapped on the door.

She called out in a clear voice, "Nothing serious."

Then she turned a tear-streaked face ravaged by grief toward him. "It won't be okay. It can't. He has my daughter."

He cupped her face with his hands. "Tell me. Tell me about your daughter and we'll get her back."

She drew in a shuddering breath that racked her entire body. "She's eight. I had her when I was a teenager. My father forced me to give her up—no...I gave her up willingly. He didn't have to force me. She was an inconvenience to me at that age. I got pregnant in Italy. Maddie's father was a race-car driver. He—he died in an accident, and my father instructed me to leave the country without telling Paulo's family."

She started sobbing and couldn't continue.

He swept away her stream of tears with this thumbs. "So you did the right thing and adopted her out to a loving family. Is she here in the city?"

"Yes, but you heard him. They have her. They must've found out about her from my laptop, the laptop they stole from my condo. I had pictures of her on that computer." She turned her father's laptop toward her. "And here. My father had pictures of her, too. I couldn't believe it when I saw them. He must've had someone taking pictures of her all along, but he never showed them to me. He must've figured I didn't care."

"Maybe he didn't want to upset you." He rubbed a hand down her arm, wishing like hell he could take away the pain etched into grooves on her face.

"Can you verify her…kidnapping with her parents?"

"I'm not in touch with them. If I tell them now this is all my fault, that they lost their daughter because of me, they'll hate me. Besides, you saw her picture. She was holding a copy of today's newspaper. They have her."

He pulled her head against his chest. "You didn't do anything wrong, London. He's not going to hurt Maddie. If he did, he'd have no leverage over you. He's just showing you that he can get to her."

Judd stopped stroking her hair, and a deep worry permeated his bones.

London looked up at him. "What's wrong? If I don't pursue this anymore, they'll leave her alone, right?"

He brushed her hair from her damp face and stared out the window. "Twenty years ago, when my father was going through hell, my brother Eric was kidnapped."

London sniffed. "He survived."

"He did. At the time, people said it was a sympathy ploy and a diversion for my father. They believed he planned the kidnapping himself."

"No parent would do that."

"It was the same as your daughter, London. They were proving to my father that they could get to his family. He knew. He knew he was being set up and he knew who was responsible. That's why he never said anything. They threatened us. They threatened his family. It's the same despicable bunch now."

Her hands fisted in her lap. "How are we going to get her back? How are we going to stop them?"

"We've got to put an end to this right now." He wiped her face with his T-shirt. "He made a mistake. He gave something away—Operation Phoenix."

"What is that?"

"Look." He tapped the laptop, bringing it to life. "I searched for Operation Phoenix while he was talking to you and got some hits."

London trapped her hands between her knees. "I'm afraid to know."

"No, you're not." He rubbed her back. "I know you want to get that little girl back to her family."

She squeezed her eyes shut and drew in a deep breath as if she were drawing upon some well of strength to face her fears.

He started opening the files and folders, and they began to piece together the story of Operation Phoenix.

"These figures are bad." She poked at the monitor. "BGE was facing some lean times twenty-five years ago, and then like magic our fortunes turned around."

"Look at these shipments." He ran his finger down the columns of a spreadsheet. "Pharmaceuticals, methylene."

She leaned closer. "BGE hasn't been in pharma for years."

"It looks as if this is where it started, London, but there doesn't seem to be any target location for these shipments."

"So where did all that methylene go?"

It took them skimming through a few more files, but Judd found what he was looking for. "Bogus companies, bogus addresses. All this methylene was ending up on the street as crystal."

"Meth?" She folded her arms across her stomach. "You mean BGE was supplying drug dealers. We made hundreds of millions of dollars from these shipments."

"That's what it looks like. My father and his partner must've suspected something when this stuff started showing up on the streets."

"I think I'm going to be sick." She cupped her hands over her mouth and nose and took deep breaths in and out. "I can't believe my father would do this."

"He may not have known." He flicked his finger at the monitor. "Look at all these scanned invoices. That's not your father's name, unless he used his middle name or something for signing off."

She squinted at the screen. "That's my uncle Jay's signature."

"Is that Niles's father?"

"Yes." She gripped the edge of the desk. "Are you trying to tell me my uncle Jay engineered the setup of your father and his partner because they found out about his side business? My uncle died years ago, after my father pushed him out of the company. So who's been stirring up trouble since then? Who's been trying to keep your brothers from discovering the truth? And who has Maddie?"

"Niles is the obvious suspect. And if that's the case, I don't believe he's working alone." He tapped the desk with the end of a pen. "He's a member of the Bohemian Club up on Nob Hill, isn't he?"

"Y-yes. I just told you the other day that my father was a member, too, and Uncle Jay."

"I've had clients who were members. One tried to blindfold me when he took me there, but I pointed out I wouldn't be able to do my job blindfolded."

"So they allowed a nonmember into the club? Did you witness any of their silly rituals?"

"He invited me in as a guest, which is allowed, and there were no rituals that night. But I did get an eyeful."

"Is it true there are nude, masked women lounging around the club?"

"Not that night, but I did see a few city movers and shakers, including a couple of high-ranking police officials. Anyone else may not have recognized them, but since my brother is a detective I knew who they were."

"What are you implying, Judd?"

"I'm connecting the dots. Your father's company was involved in illegal activities, whether he knew about those activities or not, and there had to be a lot of cover-up of those activities. Your father was also a big supporter of law enforcement. He was on the police commission."

"It's like we said before—who else but the police would be able to plant that evidence on your father? Who else could get to so many people so easily? But who do you think is involved? It can't be the chief of police. He's relatively new to the city."

"But there are others. Others who were around then and are around today. Others who don't want any of this to come out, any more than Niles does."

He reached for his cell phone. "I'm calling my brother Sean. He's been on his leave of absence long enough. We need his help."

"And what about Eric? You said he worked on the FBI's child-abduction task force. He was abducted himself— probably by these same people."

"I think Eric's in D.C., but he'll come out for this." He snapped his fingers. "And Ryan. I'm calling him down here from Crestview. He knows Cynthia. He spoke to the real

Phone Book Killer. We're going to put this together, and we're going to get Maddie safely home to her family and ensure her future security and yours."

She grabbed his hand and squeezed it so hard he heard his bones crack. "I gave her up to give her a secure life. As her birth mother, I owe her that."

"They won't hurt her. If they do, they know there's nothing stopping you from spilling everything you've discovered. They won't risk that."

"But once they find out we know it all, every sickening detail, they'll have nothing to lose by hurting her."

"Look at me." He took her chin between his fingers and stared into her green eyes, glassy with fear. "Nothing is going to happen to you or Maddie, not as long as I have breath in my body."

"When do you think he's going to call back?"

"When he's good and ready. That's the point, to show his strength and power. But we have work to do in the meantime."

LATER THAT NIGHT, back at her place, London paced the floor, cupping her phone in her hands. Judd's two brothers in California, Sean and Ryan, were already on their way to the city. Ryan might have already arrived. And Eric was taking the first flight out of D.C. Judd's plan had to work. She hadn't given up her baby all those years ago only to put her in mortal danger now.

The company she'd been trying so hard to be worthy of now sickened her. She wanted to believe it was all Uncle Jay's doing. It hadn't been too long after Joseph Brody's suicide that Spencer had pushed Jay out of BGE. If her father had been completely complicit in the illegal activities, he wouldn't have been able to do that. Jay wouldn't have allowed it. Her uncle probably would've used her father's involvement to gain a bigger foothold in the company—for himself and his son.

She had to hang on to that.

The phone vibrated in her hand and she checked the display. She nodded at Judd and put the phone on speaker.

"Hi, Niles. Thanks for getting back to me."

"Of course. You piqued my curiosity."

"I want you to come to my place so I can talk to you face-to-face and give you some paperwork, but the upshot is I want to step down as CEO of BGE."

He sucked in his breath, and his excitement was palpable over the phone. "I'm having dinner near Union Square. I can be there in a jiffy."

She ended the call and pocketed the phone. "So he's on his way."

"He's gonna wish he'd stayed in Union Square." Judd's eyes narrowed and the menace rolled off him in waves.

They finalized their plans and Judd relocated to the burned-out unit next door while she waited for Niles's arrival.

London paced the room until the buzzer on her intercom filled the room. "Yes?"

"What do you mean, yes? It's Niles."

"Okay, I'm letting you in, but you still need to check in with the security guard in the lobby—new policy."

She waited a few seconds and slipped out of her place. She jogged down the hallway and tapped once on the door to the empty unit.

Judd let her in. "Are you ready?"

"As ready as I'll ever be to detain and torture my cousin."

"Nobody's getting tortured." He placed his hand at the back of her neck and massaged the base of her skull with his thumb. "Just remember what he's been doing."

"Allegedly."

"Are you chickening out now?"

The sound of the elevator opening gave her renewed resolve.

"No."

She poked her head out the door. "I'm down here, Niles. Had to take care of a few things."

His gait faltered but he continued. "Can I just wait in your place?"

"It's locked up. We'll just talk here for a bit and then we'll go to my place, have a little wine and celebrate."

He brushed a lock of blond hair back from his high forehead. "I have allergies, you know. I may not be able to last too long in there."

"It won't be long, Niles." *Just until Maddie is back home safely.* She widened the door and stepped back.

He walked in, his nose wrinkling. "What are you doing in here anyway?"

Judd wasted no time. From his hiding place behind the door, he lunged at Niles and immobilized him. Then he forced him into the waiting straight-backed chair and tied him up before Niles recovered from the first assault.

Struggling against his restraints, Niles shook his head. "What is going on? Is this some kind of joke, London? This is too much, even for you."

Judd stepped in front of him, and Niles's eyes bugged out. "Wh-what are you doing here? What is this, London?"

"This—" Judd drew up another chair, facing Niles "—is an interrogation."

Niles sputtered. "This is an outrage. I'll have you arrested. I'll have your license. I know people."

"Funny you should mention those people now, because we're interested in those very people."

Niles's face drained of what little color it had. "Is this a joke, London?"

"Where's Maddie?"

"Who?" Niles ran his tongue around the outside of his mouth.

"My daughter."

Niles laughed, but it came out a croak. "You're crazy. You don't have a daughter."

"You know all about Maddie, the baby I gave up for adoption when I was a teenager. You saw her pictures on the laptop you had stolen from my condo. Did you know the men you'd hired for that job were killers?"

Niles's mouth gaped open like a fish on a line. "You've finally lost it, London. Nobody thought you were suitable to be CEO of Breck Global, but we didn't think you were crazy."

Judd rose from his chair, lifted it and then clumped it back on the floor. "Cut it. We know all about the methylene shipments organized by your father to save BGE. We know my father and his partner discovered that BGE was supplying meth labs with the stuff and maybe even went to their superiors. And we know what happened to both of them after that fact—everyone knows what happened to them."

"Meth labs? You're as crazy as London, both of you caught up in some insane conspiracy theory."

"Save it, Niles." She pulled her father's laptop out of her briefcase. "It's on here. This is what you and your father tried to find all those years, isn't it? The proof. This is what you've been looking for—Operation Phoenix—all here. My father made sure of it, made sure he had proof."

Niles slumped in his seat. "My father may have been involved in some illegal activity, but it saved the company. It was your father's company and he didn't have what it took to keep it solvent, and then he pushed Dad out."

"You mean he kept it solvent by getting involved in the drug trade?"

"What do you want from me, London? You have the

company, just like your father always wanted. I always knew he was going to cut me out, just like he cut out Dad."

"Are you going to deny that you know your cohorts kidnapped my daughter to force my hand?"

"I thought he might try something like this." He closed his eyes. "He's desperate and it's been coming for a long while, ever since that psychopath fingerprint tech decided to mimic the Phone Book Killer and get Detective Sean Brody all riled up again."

"The threats to London began after that."

"It was a perfect storm, wasn't it? He knew Spencer Breck had the proof. My father told him that his brother had the proof, and when Spencer died that proof would go to London. Who knew she would hook up with you? Who knew the real Phone Book Killer would step out of the shadows and confess? Who knew the witches' covens in this city would be put on edge by someone trying to get the power of *Los Brujos de Invierno*."

Judd jumped up, knocking his chair to the floor. "What does that coven have to do with this? My brother believes they were responsible for his kidnapping all those years ago."

"He's right. It's all linked." Niles shook his head almost sadly. "Don't you know that by now?"

London took a turn around the room. "You keep mentioning someone, but not by name. Who is it? Who has Maddie?"

"If I tell you, he'll have me killed. He's had others killed for less."

Judd put his face close to Niles's. "He's not going to have that chance. We're going to take him down. We know he's SFPD. He has to be. Again, the proof is in the files on the laptop. We'll put it together eventually, but you could tell us now and do yourself a favor."

"Or what? You have no proof against me of anything."

"We'll set you loose and put the word out on the street that you're talking. How long do you think you'll have before he silences you?"

Nile's Adam's apple bobbed in his throat. "Y-you wouldn't do that. Once you release me from here, I'm probably a dead man anyway."

"Who says we're releasing you from here, Niles?" Judd rolled up his sleeves, the tattoos on his arm snaking up his skin.

"You can't keep me prisoner."

London took Judd's place in the chair facing Niles. "That's exactly what we're going to do—until we get Maddie back to her family and shine a light on this whole sordid affair so that it can't ruin anyone else's life."

"You don't have to worry about Maddie. He's not going to harm her."

Judd growled. "It's only a matter of time before Spencer Breck's files reveal his identity, and he's never going to harm anyone again."

"Give him up, Niles. It'll go easier on you."

London glanced at Judd, who had retreated to the window. He seemed transfixed by the view.

"Judd?"

"I know who it is. He was around twenty years ago, around my father, around yours. He's a member of that club." He jabbed his finger at the glass. "The Bohemian Club. I saw him there."

Niles sputtered and sobbed.

London joined Judd at the window and took his hand. "It's Captain Williams, isn't it?"

Niles groaned from his chair.

Judd nodded at Niles. "There's your answer."

THE FOLLOWING MORNING, the four Brody brothers were scattered across her great room. They'd dropped everything they were doing to help when Judd called. Their intensity permeated the room, the very air thick with their sense of purpose and justice.

Eric, the FBI agent, perched on a stool at the kitchen island. "I told Christina everything last night, and she's convinced Williams is a member of the coven of witches who was responsible for my kidnapping. Members of that coven had definitely infiltrated the Bohemian Club—they're all about power, and he used his connections twenty years ago to have me kidnapped."

London turned to Judd's eldest brother. "Sean, what about you? You worked with Williams."

"He's always been careful to give me what I wanted and needed on the job. Maybe he didn't want to raise my suspicions." He took a sip of coffee. "Ah, about the man in the next unit. You can't hold him, Judd."

Judd snorted. "What are you going to do, arrest me? At this point we're keeping him for his own safety. If Williams finds out we're on to him, Niles is a dead man."

"He won't find out until we want him to." Ryan sat next to London and took her hand in his. "Once we get Maddie back to her home, we'll move in on Williams. He won't know what hit him."

Sean said, "I have a couple of officers with Maddie's parents, the Dillons, right now. They know nothing about the kidnappers' real motives and are waiting for the ransom note."

Judd started. "Williams?"

"Knows nothing about it. These are two guys who owe me a favor."

"I thought you didn't roll like that, bro." Judd winked at Ryan.

"Do the Dillons know these men are cops?" London twisted her fingers in her lap. Her heart ached for Maddie's parents.

"The Dillons don't know they're cops since the kidnappers' note warned them against calling the police. They just know they were sent to help and, knowing their daughter's biological mother, the offer didn't surprise them."

"We've never—I've never interfered before. The Dillons made it clear to my father that they wanted to provide for their daughter themselves, so no secret trust funds or surprise inheritances."

Judd leaned over the back of her chair and massaged her shoulders. "This is different. I'm sure they appreciate the help and concern."

A cell phone rang, and everyone checked their pockets. Sean held his up and then answered it. "Yeah? Yeah? Is she okay?" He flashed the room a thumbs-up. "That's great. Thanks, guys."

London bounded to her feet. "Is it Maddie? Is she okay?"

"Safe and sound and on her way home."

Judd crushed her in a hug.

Eric said, "Let me guess. Someone dropped her off on a street corner?"

"In a park."

"He kept his promise." London rested her head against Judd's shoulder. "He released her unharmed."

Ryan shook his head. "Now he thinks he's got you where he wants you. He's demonstrated his power and control, and if you step out of line again, he has the means to punish you."

Judd kissed the top of her head and stood tall, squaring his shoulders. "That's before the Brodys got to town—all of them."

They drove in a caravan through the city streets to the SFPD metro division, with London and Judd in the lead on his Harley. Ryan was riding with Sean in his unmarked police car and Eric brought up the rear in his rental.

The five of them trooped through the homicide division

and squeezed into the elevator up to Williams's office. The brothers didn't want to take any chances with any one of them confronting Williams on his own.

When Williams saw them through the window of his office, his face told London everything she needed to know. His face red, his dark eyes darting from Brody to Brody, Williams stammered, "Wh-what's going on? To what do I owe this pleasure? London?"

"Just stop, Captain. We know everything. I know you were behind all the threats against me, and I know you kidnapped my daughter." She patted her briefcase. "I found my father's laptop that has a trail of BGE's involvement in the drug trade and how certain members of the SFPD were complicit in covering it up in exchange for money and positions of power."

He laughed, but it was a hollow sound. "That's insane. Sean, you don't believe any of these ravings, do you?"

"I saw the proof of the involvement by certain officers, and it sickened me."

Williams jumped on their vague accusations. "Certain officers, but not me. My name's not in there, is it?"

Judd widened his stance. "We also have information from Niles Breck."

"That fool?" Williams rolled his shoulders and some of the tension left his face. "You have nothing. I don't know what you're talking about. If your cousin threatened you, London, he's just trying to implicate others now. You have no proof—none of you."

"How about me, Williams? I have proof."

Williams choked and staggered against the doorjamb of his office.

London spun around as the brothers turned slowly.

A tall, lean man with silver streaks through his black hair folded his arms and leaned against a desk.

Sean grabbed the edge of a table. "Dad."

Epilogue

London wrapped her arms around Judd's waist and smiled at the chaos in her condo. It had been Brody, Brody, Brody 24/7 the past few weeks, and of course they'd all congregated at her place, because there were so many of them and Sean's place was small and Judd's even smaller.

And all the activity swirled around a resurrected Joseph Brody, a man who had pretended to jump from a bridge twenty years ago to save his family from the inexorable menace that had closed in on him.

The brothers had forgiven him because to a one, they would've done something similar to protect their loved ones.

Marie Giardano, the records clerk, had come back from her extended vacation, a vacation she'd taken when she realized someone at the police station had been watching and following her.

Now she had her arm linked with Sean's as she shook her finger in Ryan's face, reclaiming her role as the brothers' surrogate mother.

Cynthia Phelps sat on the arm of the couch next to Judd's father, her hand resting lightly on his shoulder. She'd aided and abetted the disappearance of the man who had become her hero. He'd saved her once and she'd returned the favor by saving him. When he'd returned to San Francisco after a twenty-year absence, when he thought he could safely re-join his family, Cynthia had again been there for him, act-ing as a conduit for the two people who could sort out the lies and deceptions that had affected them both.

London whispered in Judd's ear, "Do you think your father and Cynthia could be an item?"

"You think because she played matchmaker you can return the favor?" He touched her nose and followed it with a kiss.

Joey Brody called to her, "London, it looks like BGE is going to weather the bad publicity, since your uncle was the real culprit and your father pushed him out of the com-pany years ago."

"I think the company is in good hands with my half brother, Wade. He'll right the ship, and Niles is working out a deal with the D.A. He'll do his time and hopefully learn a lesson."

Christina, Eric's fiancée, strolled across the room and gave London a hug. "Your daughter is fine now? No ill ef-fects?"

"I spoke to her parents on the phone, and she's doing well. Nobody harmed her physically and the kidnappers didn't try to frighten her."

"I'm so happy to hear that."

London's gaze wandered to Christina's daughter loung-ing in Eric's lap. "Kendall is adorable."

"She's a handful, but she's happy to have her daddy in her life."

"And he looks happy to be there."

Ryan came up behind Judd and smacked him on the back. "I think it's pretty awesome that you of all people figured it all out in the end."

Judd turned to his brother. "I didn't figure it all out. Re-ally, we didn't have any proof against Williams except for Niles's confession. Williams's name still hasn't come up in Spencer Breck's notes and documents on that laptop. It was all Dad, wasn't it? When Williams saw that ghost from his past, he gave it all up."

Kacie Manning, Ryan's girlfriend, joined their group, handing Ryan a beer. "It's an amazing story."

London nodded. "We couldn't have gotten as far as we did without Joey's help. He got Cynthia to get me and Judd together, and then he left the newspaper clipping on Judd's motorcycle and even convinced Otis Branch's cell mate to contact Judd."

Kacie swiveled her head toward the Brody patriarch and bit her lip. "This would be an incredible book, Ryan. Do you think all your brothers would approve?"

Ryan kissed her hand. "I think we need to give this story a rest for now. How about you revisit it in another twenty years?"

Sean held up a glass and tapped it with a fork. "Can I get everyone's attention?"

Eric jumped up and yelled, "Dad's back from the dead. You can sit down now, Sean."

The room erupted in laughter and Sean rolled his eyes at Elise Duran, his fiancée and the woman he'd rescued from a serial killer. "I just want to thank London for her hospitality. I want to thank Cynthia for everything she's done for Dad, and I want to give thanks for having Dad back in our lives after all these years. And finally, I want to thank the three best brothers a man could ever ask for."

Tears were streaming down Elise's face by the end of Sean's speech, and she threw her arms around his neck while everyone clapped and whistled.

Judd pulled London close and whispered in her ear, "Let's blow this joint."

"But this is my joint."

He raised an eyebrow as that lock of black hair fell over his eye. "Are you a CEO or a free spirit?"

Excitement fizzed through her veins as it always would when she looked into the blue eyes of the man she loved.

She tapped her own glass. "My turn. It's been wonderful having you all here, and I've been so honored to be part of this fantastic reunion. Please continue to make yourselves at home, and just lock up behind you whenever you leave."

"And where are you two going?" Joseph Brody stood up, his three eldest sons around him.

Judd met his father's eyes. "It's time for us to hit the road."

Joseph Brody dipped his head once. "You be careful out there, son."

Outside, London snuggled up against Judd's back on the Harley. "Where are we going?"

"Does it matter?"

"Not as long as I'm with you."

He revved the engine. "That's the answer I've been looking for, London Breck."

She rested her chin on his shoulder. "And you're the man I've been looking for, Judd Brody."

As Judd crested the next hill, she tapped him on the shoulder and pointed at the horizon, the Golden Gate Bridge outlined against an orange sky.

Then they really did ride off into the sunset.

* * * * *

COMING NEXT MONTH FROM

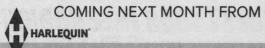

HARLEQUIN®

INTRIGUE

Available October 21, 2014

#1527 RUSTLING UP TROUBLE
Sweetwater Ranch • by Delores Fossen
Deputy Rayanne McKinnon believes ATF agent Blue McCurdy, father to her unborn child, is dead—until he shows up with hired killers on his trail and no memory of their night together.

#1528 THE HUNK NEXT DOOR
The Specialists • by Debra Webb & Regan Black
Fearless Police Chief Abigail Jensen seized a drug shipment, halting the cash flow of an embedded terrorist cell. Can undercover specialist Riley O'Brien find the threat before the terrorists retaliate?

#1529 BONEYARD RIDGE
The Gates • by Paula Graves
To save her from a deadly ambush, undercover P.I. Hunter Bragg takes Susannah Marsh on the run. But when their escape alerts a dangerous enemy from Susannah's past, Hunter will need to rely on the other members of The Gates to rescue the woman who healed his heart.

#1530 CROSSFIRE CHRISTMAS
The Precinct • by Julie Miller
When injured undercover cop Charlie Nash kidnapped nurse Teresa Rodriguez to stitch up his wounds, he never meant to put his brave rescuer in danger...or fall in love with her.

#1531 COLD CASE AT COBRA CREEK
by Rita Herron
Someone in town will do anything to stop Sage Freeport from getting the truth about her missing son. Tracker Dugan Graystone's offer to help is Sage's best chance to find her child...and lose her heart....

#1532 NIGHT OF THE RAVEN
by Jenna Ryan
When an old curse is recreated by someone seeking revenge, only Ethan McVey, the mysterious new Raven's Cove police chief, stands between Amara Bellam and a brutal killer.

YOU CAN FIND MORE INFORMATION ON UPCOMING HARLEQUIN® TITLES, FREE EXCERPTS AND MORE AT WWW.HARLEQUIN.COM.

HICNM1014

REQUEST YOUR FREE BOOKS!
2 FREE NOVELS PLUS 2 FREE GIFTS!

HARLEQUIN

INTRIGUE

BREATHTAKING ROMANTIC SUSPENSE

YES! Please send me 2 FREE Harlequin Intrigue® novels and my 2 FREE gifts (gifts are worth about $10). After receiving them, if I don't wish to receive any more books, I can return the shipping statement marked "cancel." If I don't cancel, I will receive 6 brand-new novels every month and be billed just $4.74 per book in the U.S. or $5.24 per book in Canada. That's a savings of at least 14% off the cover price! It's quite a bargain! Shipping and handling is just 50¢ per book in the U.S. and 75¢ per book in Canada.* I understand that accepting the 2 free books and gifts places me under no obligation to buy anything. I can always return a shipment and cancel at any time. Even if I never buy another book, the two free books and gifts are mine to keep forever.

182/382 HDN F42N

Name	(PLEASE PRINT)

Address		Apt. #

City	State/Prov.	Zip/Postal Code

Signature (if under 18, a parent or guardian must sign)

Mail to the **Harlequin® Reader Service:**
IN U.S.A.: P.O. Box 1867, Buffalo, NY 14240-1867
IN CANADA: P.O. Box 609, Fort Erie, Ontario L2A 5X3
**Are you a subscriber to Harlequin Intrigue books
and want to receive the larger-print edition?
Call 1-800-873-8635 or visit www.ReaderService.com.**

* Terms and prices subject to change without notice. Prices do not include applicable taxes. Sales tax applicable in N.Y. Canadian residents will be charged applicable taxes. Offer not valid in Quebec. This offer is limited to one order per household. Not valid for current subscribers to Harlequin Intrigue books. All orders subject to credit approval. Credit or debit balances in a customer's account(s) may be offset by any other outstanding balance owed by or to the customer. Please allow 4 to 6 weeks for delivery. Offer available while quantities last.

Your Privacy—The Harlequin® Reader Service is committed to protecting your privacy. Our Privacy Policy is available online at www.ReaderService.com or upon request from the Harlequin Reader Service.

We make a portion of our mailing list available to reputable third parties that offer products we believe may interest you. If you prefer that we not exchange your name with third parties, or if you wish to clarify or modify your communication preferences, please visit us at www.ReaderService.com/consumerschoice or write to us at Harlequin Reader Service Preference Service, P.O. Box 9062, Buffalo, NY 14269. Include your complete name and address.

HI13R

SPECIAL EXCERPT FROM

HARLEQUIN®

I N T R I G U E®

*A surprise attack on her family ranch reunites a pregnant
deputy with her baby's father—who supposedly died five
months ago...*

Read on for an excerpt from
RUSTLING UP TROUBLE
by USA TODAY bestselling author

Delores Fossen

She put her hand on his back to steady him. Bare skin on bare skin.

The hospital gown hardly qualified as a garment, with one side completely off his bandaged shoulder. Judging from the drafts he felt on various parts of his body, Rayanne was probably getting an eyeful.

Of course, it apparently wasn't something she hadn't already seen, since according to her they'd slept together five months ago.

"Will saying I'm sorry help?" he mumbled, and because he had no choice, he ditched the bargaining-position idea and lay back down.

"Nothing will help. As soon as you're back on your feet, I want you out of Sweetwater Springs and miles and miles away from McKinnon land. Got that?"

Oh, yeah. It was crystal clear.

It didn't matter that he didn't know why he'd done the things he had, but he'd screwed up. Maybe soon, Blue would remember everything that he might be trying to forget.

Her phone rang, the sound shooting through the room. And his head. Rayanne fished the phone from her pocket, looked at the screen and then moved to the other side of the room to take the call. It occurred to him then that she might be involved with someone.

Five months was a long time.

And this someone might be calling to make sure she was okay.

Blue felt the twinge of jealousy that throbbed right along with the pain in various parts of his body, and he wished he could just wake up from this crazy nightmare that he was having.

"No, he doesn't remember," she said to whoever had called. She turned to look back at him, but her coat shifted to the side.

Just enough for Blue to see the stomach bulge beneath her clothes.

Oh, man.

It felt as if someone had sucked the air right out of his lungs. He didn't need his memory to understand what that meant.

Rayanne was pregnant.

Find out how Rayanne reacts to Blue's discovery and what they plan to do to protect their unborn child when
RUSTLING UP TROUBLE
by USA TODAY bestselling author
Delores Fossen hits shelves in November 2014.

HARLEQUIN®
INTRIGUE®

READ THE FINAL INSTALLMENT OF JULIE MILLER'S GRIPPING MINISERIES *THE PRECINCT: TASK FORCE*

With his life bleeding out from bullet wounds and a car crash, Charles Nash's best option is to kidnap the innocent nurse who stops to help him. At gunpoint, the jaded DEA undercover agent offers Teresa Rodriguez a desperate deal: if she keeps him alive long enough to find out who's blown his cover and set him up to die, she'll be home for Christmas.

But can he keep that promise?

As the two go on the run from an unknown killer, the Good Samaritan gives Nash a bad case of unprofessional desire. He's drawn to the sexy little spitfire for her bravery, boldness and attitude. But he won't count on kissing her under mistletoe. The cartel thugs after Nash want them both dead!

CROSSFIRE CHRISTMAS
BY JULIE MILLER

Only from Harlequin® Intrigue®.
Available November 2014
wherever books and ebooks are sold.